A Bite of the Apple
Portal Adventures Book 1

Joyce Hertzoff

Susan, Happy Reading

Joyce Hertzoff

ISBN: 153704222X
ISBN-13: 978-1537042220

DEDICATION

To Ira for his patience and understanding. To critiquers at
Writers Village University, and my fantasy group, Kathy
Wagoner and Carol March. And to my beta, Aya Walksfar.
Thank you all.

CHAPTER 1.

I dreamed of being anywhere other than the farm where I'd lived all my life with my parents and younger brother. I wiped perspiration from my brow and pushed an errant hair from my eyes. Long sleeves protected fair skin, inherited from my mother. My blouse stuck to my back. My knees and fingers ached. So many weeds! Where had they all come from? Even with the excessive spring rains, I hadn't expected to have to pull so many. I'd already filled one burlap sack. I wasn't complaining.

"Bet, bring me some carrots and munstels, please." My mother's voice reached me all the way from the house.

I stopped weeding long enough to pull four long orange roots and pluck a dozen of the tan fungi from the ground. The weather that produced the weeds also gave us a bumper crop of vegetables. Poppa took a wagon load into Romik that morning to sell at the marketplace.

I stretched my legs and fingers before walking the

short distance to the back door of our one-story farmhouse and entered the kitchen.

Momma took the vegetables. "I hope your father's delayed because he sold most of our crops."

If he sold enough we could go on a holiday. Every time Aunt Gillian returned from a trip and regaled us with stories of far-off lands, I dreamed of traveling myself, but I had never gone far from home.

The sun hadn't progressed much further across the sky when the clip-clop of horses filled the air. Poppa approached in the horse-drawn wagon. Aunt Gill rode beside him.

She wore one of her elegant riding costumes, a red fitted short coat over a long full skirt in a soft gray fabric. She'd arranged her golden hair in lovely coils on top of her head, making her appear even taller.

"Aunt Gill!" Ian rushed out to greet them both and assist our aunt to dismount.

At nineteen I was too old for such exuberance, but then again, my brother had always been more boisterous than I. Still, I couldn't refrain from grinning at the sight of her.

Ian helped Poppa unhitch the wagon. I led the steeds to the corral and returned immediately.

"What did you bring?" Ian sounded even younger than his sixteen years.

"Ian! Your manners!" I scolded, but Aunt Gill

laughed. She always brought the most exotic gifts: silk scarves and handkerchiefs from Plum Island in the Inland Sea, chocolates from the mountains of Gorsland, painted clay pots from the sandy deserts of Panea, and seashell necklaces from beaches up and down a far off coast. Would I ever see those places?

"Wait until you see what I have for you both!" she teased. We frowned, knowing we would have to be patient until after dinner.

As Ian walked to the house with Aunt Gill, I helped my father unload the wagon.

He took off his straw hat and wiped his wide brow with a plaid cloth. "The new tavern owner purchased most of our vegetables and I had a steady stream of people wanting our peaches and plums." He jiggled a pouch of coins. His grin reached his warm brown eyes. I loved Poppa's eyes and wished I'd gotten them instead of my washed out blues.

We took the remaining produce to the kitchen. By the time Poppa and Aunt Gill had cleaned off the road dust from their hands and faces, Momma had dinner on our sturdy wood table. Besides chicken stew, we had a salad of greens and a hearty bread she baked that afternoon. Poppa dished out the food.

My parents' always insisted we hold our conversation until we were at least half-way through our meal. As we ate, I noticed Aunt Gillian's eyes stray from her plate to me a few times. Each time, a smile crossed her lips. What did she want to say to me? What was she thinking?

Ian never ate so fast. "Where did you go this time?" he asked our aunt as soon as she ate half her food.

Aunt Gill smiled as she swallowed. "Bonafilina. It's a beautiful jungle land, filled with colorful birds and flowers, trees that reach towards the sky, and a people with very brown skin."

Ian's eyes went wide. Aunt Gill's descriptions entranced me too. She told us about the exotic customs of the people and the foods they served. Then Momma brought out the apple pie she'd baked that day.

"But nothing I ate in Bonafilina could compare to your food, Charlotte," Aunt Gill told her.

"Oh, go on!" Momma patted her sister's hand. "You're just saying that."

"It's true!" She ate every morsel of her pie, then put down her fork. "And to thank you for such a wonderful meal, I'll wash up. Bet, why don't you help me?"

"Afterward, can we open our presents?" Ian voice held a plaintive note.

"Yes, of course." Gill smiled at him.

While Ian and Poppa went to see to the animals for the evening, and Momma relaxed in her rocker with her needlepoint, I helped my aunt clear the table and then filled a basin with water from the pump. I warmed it for a while on the hearth, then used a cake of soap to scrub the plates, forks and other utensils.

"Have you ever wondered why I travel so much?" Aunt Gill asked in a low voice as we worked side-by-side.

I sensed her eyes on me. "I thought it was because you found it enlightening and enjoyable." Glancing at her out of the corner of my eye, I rolled up my sleeves, but they were already wet with soap suds.

"Well, it is that, surely. But I don't travel only for pleasure." She paused as if unsure how to say something. "I'm sent by the Council."

"The High Council?" My voice squeaked in surprise. They'd ruled the land since democracy replaced the monarchy in our country more than a hundred years before. "What can you do for them?"

"Oh, a bit of this and a bit of that." She waved a hand vaguely.

I waited to see whether she'd say more, and eventually she did. "Often I act as a courier, carrying letters that cannot go through official channels."

"Oh!" That sounded infinitely more exciting than traveling only to see the sights. "I bet you've met the most interesting people!"

"Yes, yes, I have." She hesitated. What had she chosen to leave out?

"Go on." I forgot I had two dirty knives in my hands and stared at her.

She studied my face before she continued. "There are times when my task is more dangerous." She said the next slowly, perhaps to be certain I understood the gravity. "I'm sent to obtain information our government needs. Or explore a place we've never visited before. Sometimes to establish a relationship with their government." I must have looked stricken because she added, "I've been well-trained for my work, as you will be."

"Me?" The knives clattered as they fell into the basin.

Aunt Gill sighed. "I'm not getting any younger. It's time to prepare my successor. I've proposed you to the council as my replacement."

I shook my head. "What do I know about these things? I've never been farther away from home than Romik except the two times we went to the seashore at Cobend. I...I grow vegetables and tend to animals."

She nodded. "And so you must be trained. You'll return with me to the capital, and we'll begin your education."

"But the summer crops! Molly is almost ready to calve!" Everything I had to do at the farm flew through my mind.

"Your parents and Ian can manage without you. Your conscientiousness make you more suitable than you know."

"Have you asked them? My parents I mean."

"I don't need their permission: you're of age. I'll discuss it with them, but you're the one who'll have to make the decision."

How could I? "I'll travel all over? See some of the places you've told us about?" My hands trembled with excitement.

"Yes, and more." She stilled my hands, wet from the dishwater. "Give it some thought. I believe you won't disappoint me. I know you can do this, Bet."

After she said that, did I have a choice? I barely registered the beauty of the shawls Aunt Gill brought for Momma and me, or the leather pouches for Poppa and Ian. My mind was too full of speculation, doubts and anticipation.

That night when I changed into my nightgown and slid under the quilt my mother had crocheted when I was twelve, my mind was awhirl. I thought about what I'd miss besides my family: the smell of newly turned soil, the first seedlings peeking through, the heady scent of spring blossoms on the fruit trees, and the crisp, sweet taste of the first apples. Did the lure of adventure surpass the life I had on the farm?

One moment my heart pounded with the excitement of traveling, meeting strange and wonderful people, the kind I'd only known through Aunt Gill's stories. The very next, dread settled heavily on my chest, keeping me from breathing.

In the morning, tired from a night tossing in my bed, I knew what my answer had to be. I swallowed my fears and reservations, but I had to take a chance, to see the world and all it held. Then I could come home, content to spend the rest of my life here.

I washed and dressed before I joined my family for breakfast. As I neared the kitchen, I heard my parents and Aunt Gillian arguing.

"What does she know about how you travel?" Momma sounded angry.

Gill spoke in her normal calm voice. "She'll learn, the same way I did. Charlotte, she's a grown woman. You can't keep her here on the farm for her entire life."

"How will she defend herself from the dangers out there?" Momma's voice rose.

"Her training will be very complete. I'll make sure of it myself and accompany her the first few times she journeys, give her the benefit of my own knowledge and skills. I will not let her go alone until I'm sure she's ready."

My mother caught sight of me and had the grace to blush. Not so my aunt. "Good morning, Bet. We were talking about you."

"And deciding my fate, no doubt. Whatever happened to it being my decision?" I glared at my aunt, and then at my parents.

"The final decision will be yours." Poppa's usual smile had been replaced by a tight jaw. "But I hope you realize everything you'll have to do. Traveling the way your aunt does is not all fun and romance."

I smiled at him. "I know that. Aunt Gill told me enough so I can imagine the dangers."

Momma frowned. "It sounds as if you've seriously considered my sister's proposal."

"What's happened?" Ian burst into the kitchen. "I could hear your voices at the back of the house."

"Gillian asked Bet to travel with her." Mother glowered at my aunt.

"Why can't I go?"

"Because the journeys won't be for pleasure." I put a hand on my brother's shoulder. "It's..." I wasn't certain how much to tell him.

"What Bet is trying to say is I travel on government business."

Ian's brow furrowed. "What does Bet know about the government? The only thing she knows about foreign lands is what you told us."

Momma sighed. "Exactly what I said."

"Are you going, then?" Ian asked me.

The moment I nodded, my mother gasped. She would worry about me. Still, I could do nothing to calm her fears.

"Well, that's that, then." Poppa's shoulders slumped. He turned towards the door. "I'm going to feed the animals."

I would have offered to go with him, but expected he wanted to be alone with his thoughts.

"We'll leave tomorrow morning." Aunt Gill took charge.

"So soon?" It was happening too fast. A million thoughts raced through my mind from whether I could do what she did, to what one wore in the capital.

My mother must have resigned herself to my inevitable departure. "After breakfast, I can help you pick out what you should take." Or perhaps she wanted some time alone with me before I left.

But Aunt Gillian came with us, "To make sure you take appropriate clothing." As we walked from the kitchen table, Ian grumbled "And I'll have to do Bet's work as well as my own while she has an adventure."

Aunt Gill sat in the only chair in my room. "First off, show me your most elegant dress. You'll need clothing for formal occasions."

I nodded and brought out my favorite blue dress with an ankle-length, full skirt and lace at the end of the long sleeves and around the neckline.

"Is that the best thing you have?" She frowned.

"Why, yes." I glanced at my mother.

Gill sighed. "I guess I can take you shopping in Willoughby."

I pictured myself in the kind of clothing Aunt Gill wore. "How often will I have to wear dressy clothes?"

"There will be places where you'll be invited to diplomatic dinners and parties. And sometimes the council sponsors dinners in the capital."

"Oh!" I hadn't considered that. What else didn't I know?

Aunt Gill ignored my dismay and went on. "This will do for luncheons. The skirt you have on now is perfect for when you have to rough it."

"Rough it? You mean like the time you went to the land where everyone slept in tents?"

"Yes." She chuckled. "Times like those. Now, you have sturdy boots and shoes, but are there any party shoes in your closet?"

Before long, dresses and shoes covered my bed as my aunt helped me pick the 'right' ones to take. Once she finished, she stood back. "Well, these will do until we go shopping."

I surveyed all we'd chosen. "Now I have a million chores to do for the last time so I don't leave Ian with so much that he hates me."

When I joined him in the garden, and repeated what I said, he took my hands. "Oh, Bet, I could never hate you! I will miss you so much!"

I would miss him, too. Then again, with me gone, he might grow up a bit. I smiled. "I'll come home when I can."

I passed the day with my chores as always, but my

mind strayed to the way my life would change. That night, I tossed and turned in bed once more, until I finally drifted off to a restless sleep. I dreamed I stood in a large room with high ceilings. The people around me wore exquisite clothes, the men in brocade waistcoats over lace-trimmed shirts and shiny trousers, and the women in brightly-colored satin gowns, encrusted with jewels, their hair in twisted piles on top of their heads and their feet in dainty shoes. I looked down at my plain skirt, the embroidered blouse, and shoes muddy from the field.

We sat down to dinner at a long mahogany table, set with fine china, gold cutlery and snow-white table linens. I had no idea about any of the foods passed to me. When I asked the woman on my right which fork to use, she replied in a dialect I couldn't understand. I took something that looked like the seashells Aunt Gill brought us once, tried to open it, and suddenly I was transported to the shore.

I stood alone on the beach. Blue water stretched as far as I could see, and the sand burned my toes. My skin blistered in the bright sunshine and I dove into the sea to cool it, even though I had never learned to swim.

I suddenly woke, fragments of my dream lingering in my mind. It felt so real, unlike my usual dreams. A chill ran up my spine.

CHAPTER 2.

Momma insisted on preparing my favorite breakfast of eggs with cheese melted on top, fried potatoes and thick slices of ham. She wrapped some bread, cheese, carrots and apples in cloth for our journey.

"Charlotte, we won't go hungry along the way!" Aunt Gill said. "I planned to stop in Dunley and have lunch with Clare and Piers."

"Who are they?" Ian asked. "Did we ever meet them?"

Gill stared at him a minute. "No, I don't suppose you have. They are old friends of your mother's and mine."

"How long will it take to reach the capital?" I assumed we'd stay at Aunt Gill's place there, but I knew so little. How many questions could I ask?

"A good part of the day. We should arrive by nightfall."

I finished eating, but took another cup of hot tea,

not ready yet to leave the only home I'd ever known.

"Stop dawdling, Bet." Aunt Gill placed her own cup firmly on the saucer.

I took one more sip and stood. Momma hugged me tightly. "Take care of yourself and listen to everything your aunt says." A mixture of sadness and anxiety filled her moist eyes as she brushed an errant lock of blond hair from mine.

"Yes, Momma." I smiled at her and kissed her cheek. "I'll return before you know it."

"Bye, Bet." Ian pressed his lips together.

"You wish you were coming with us, don't you? Perhaps some time in the future." I rested my hand on his shoulder. "Meanwhile I'll count on you to harvest the rest of the vegetables. And look after Molly when she calves."

"Of course!"

Poppa had been quiet, but before I left the kitchen, he handed me a small but heavy pouch. It jingled with coins. "You might need this. It's some of yesterday's proceeds."

"Thank you, Poppa." I hugged him, surprised at the emotions filling me and how my voice cracked.

Aunt Gill and I took our bags out to the stable. I saddled Regis, the spotted horse I'd raised. This would be the first time I'd ridden him farther than the nearby town. He snorted at the unfamiliar weight of the saddle and bags, but didn't complain when I climbed up on his back.

Aunt Gill mounted her horse, a black stallion half a hand taller than Regis, and led the way down our lane to the road.

I allowed myself one look back at my father, mother and brother, waving to us from the doorway. Then I faced forward, hoping anew I could manage the challenges I'd have to face.

We rode through Romik. Villagers waved to us and we waved back. Once we were out in the countryside, my aunt turned to me. "You'll see many new sights on this journey to Willoughby, but none as strange as those you'll find when we're traveling."

"I'm not apprehensive about what I'll see." I sat up straight in my saddle and hoped Aunt Gill hadn't heard the slight tremble in my voice. "I only hope I won't disappoint you."

"I doubt you will."

"Aunt Gillian, what kinds of lessons will I have? Will I learn the languages of the different countries?"

"Some, although you'll find it's not necessary." She started to say something else but stopped and shook her head. "It's more important to be open to learning as you experience each new place." She hesitated before going on. "There are lands and people we know nothing about, and our travels will help us to learn about them." She fell silent again for so long I feared she would say no more. Just as I opened my mouth to ask what she meant, she said, "I haven't been completely honest with you."

I drew in my breath then wet my lips, tempted to stop my horse right there. "What do you mean?"

"You likely expect to travel by horse or on a ship to other lands of Nokar."

"Well, yes. How else is there?"

She bit her lower lip. "What we call 'portals'. Many of my journeys take me through them, not just to other lands, but to other worlds."

"Portals? You mean like doorways?" I clung to the part of what she'd said that seemed familiar, not wanting to think about what she meant by 'other worlds'.

"Yes, portals are similar to doorways or thresholds but they work by...magic. We're not completely sure how. Perhaps the council knows more than the travelers, but still not much. The first were discovered over a hundred years ago and allow us to move through time and space to other places."

My body stiffened and I blinked. I couldn't grasp everything she said. "But...but what are the portals if not doors? Magic?" Surely I'd heard her wrong.

She smiled. "They take many forms from archways to cave entrances, gates to passageways. But as long as you have a key, you can pass through. That's where the magic comes in."

"A key?" I felt like a ninny repeating my aunt's words.

She nodded. "Some are actual keys, like you would use to open a door, but many appear to be everyday objects – a coin, a piece of fruit, or a piece of paper for example."

I remembered my dream. "Or a seashell?" Glancing at my aunt, I saw a thoughtful look on her face.

Gill chuckled. "Yes, even a seashell."

"And I'll be taught how to use these keys and portals?"

"Oh, yes! That's the most important part of your training, and why you and I will go together at first. Although, sometimes we don't know where the portals will lead. That's the most exciting part."

"And the danger?"

She nodded.

We remained silent until we reached Dunley, and it gave me time to think about what Aunt Gill said. Despite my dream, I couldn't really imagine what it would be like to go through any kind of doorway and suddenly be somewhere else. Did Aunt Gill ever know beforehand what she'd find on the other side? But how could she? And where did the keys come from? In fact, where did the thresholds come from?

Dunley was much larger than Romik. The houses and shops were larger too, and there were so many more of them. People crowded the streets, walking or on horseback. Aunt Gill led me along a main avenue, but then turned down a side street. She stopped in front of a tall, narrow building with a stone front. I wasn't sure at first if it was a home or not, but the door opened and a short, blond woman came out.

Aunt Gill dismounted and the woman hugged her before Gill turned back to me. "Bet, this is Clare. Clare, this is my niece, Anabet. Charlotte's daughter."

"She resembles you both. Welcome, Bet," Clare said in a light, musical voice. "Gill has told us so much about you and your brother."

I glanced at my aunt, then we followed Clare into the small entryway. A parlor to one side contained an upholstered sofa and chairs. On the other side, a dining room held a large table in a shiny wood, surrounded by six matching chairs. Clare led us along the side of a stairway to a kitchen at the back of the house.

"You must be thirsty after your ride this morning." Clare poured us each a glass of what looked like cold tea.

I gladly took one and sipped. The cold sweet tea refreshed my dry and dusty mouth.

"I'll have lunch ready shortly. We didn't know when you'd arrive. Piers will be along momentarily. He had business to attend to."

I listened as Clare went on and on about what we'd eat and how happy she was to see us. I could listen to her musical voice for hours, whatever she said.

Some of the kitchen looked like ours on the farm, but I'd never seen some of the items on the painted wood counters. One, a tall, silver-colored pot, appeared to be in two pieces, the upper one sat on the bottom with a lid at the very top.

Clare must have seen me staring. "It's a coffeemaker."

"Coffeemaker?"

"I don't think Bet has ever had coffee," Aunt Gill said.

"We shall have some with lunch." Clare took the pieces apart. Inside were even more pieces, all the same silvery material. "One of the best discoveries we made on our journeys." She opened a pouch and scooped out a coarse brown powder, putting it into one part of the contraption. Next, she turned a knob over the sink and water came out of a spout. I'd seen something like it at the tavern in Romik. Clare filled the top half of the pot with water, placed the piece holding the grains inside the bottom half, and reassembled the entire thing. She put it on her hearth. "This will be ready before long. Sit, sit, I'll prepare lunch."

We sat, and she placed four dishes and four bowls on the table. Before she finished, a man walked into the room. Tall, towering over Clare, with black hair and a mustache, he smiled when he saw us, or at least Aunt Gill.

"Gillian, you never change!" he said.

"Oh, Piers, you are such a flatterer!"

"This must be Bet. Hello, Bet. I'm Piers, Clare's dearly beloved."

"Pleased to meet you." I didn't know what else to say.

"You look a lot like your aunt." Why would he think so? I could never look as elegant as Gill. "I see I'm just in time for lunch." He rubbed his hands together and took one of the other chairs.

Clare gave us each cutlery, placed several platters of food on the table, then she too sat. "Dig in!"

The food was familiar and yet not. Instead of the freshly harvested fruits and vegetables I ate at home there were carrots and greens, preserved in a thick liquid, and apples and pears in their own juice. The meat slices were cured. I think it was beef, but could have been pork, like smoked ham. I took a little of everything. The vegetables were vinegary and the meat salty. Perhaps I was very hungry, but every bite tasted delicious.

"Has Gill told you I used to travel, too?" Clare asked me.

"But you aren't any longer?"

"No, it was time to have a more normal life. I'd met Piers and didn't want to be away from him for long." She smiled up at him.

"Did you...did you travel to other worlds, too?" I hoped I wasn't speaking out of turn. She hadn't said Piers knew where she went, but I assumed he did. I glanced his way. He didn't seem surprised.

"So she's told you that much has she?" Clare smirked at Aunt Gill. "It's all right. We can talk about it here, although it's a topic we don't mention with others." She turned to my aunt. "Who will train Bet? Besides yourself, that is."

"Morgan, of course, and perhaps Cass."

I'd never heard of any of these people, didn't even know whether they were men or women, not from their names.

"Then she'll be thoroughly trained."

I cleared my throat. "You're both talking as if I'm not here."

Piers chuckled. "Don't mind them. When they get to chatting they forget I'm around, too."

I ate and listened, but they only spoke about friends and enemies I didn't know. I couldn't remember all the names. Clare finally stopped talking to bring out a cherry pie for dessert, admitting, "I didn't bake this myself. The bakery in town makes wonderful pastries."

Not too sweet, it brimmed with tart fruit, but it wasn't as delicious as those my mother baked. The coffee Clare served with it tasted more bitter than any tea I had ever had, and yet it had an interesting, smoky flavor, especially when Piers suggested I add sugar to it.

After lunch, Aunt Gill said, "We'd best leave now if

we want to reach the capital by nightfall."

"You'll come back again soon," Clare implored.

"Of course." My aunt hugged her and shook Piers hand. I held back at first, but Clare pulled me into her arms and whispered in my ear, "I know you'll do well." Her husband patted my shoulder, and I forced a smile.

Well-fed, Aunt Gill and I left the house and remounted. We rode through the town again and into countryside. After two or three hours, the scenery changed abruptly. Instead of fields and pastures, the road passed through one town after another, each larger than the one before, full of people and shops, everyone busy with their work. Finally, we reached the outskirts of the capital.

I'd never seen anything like it, buildings taller than the tallest trees, and streets teeming with people, horses and wagons.

"We'll go directly to my place. Tomorrow will be soon enough to take you to the council." Gill turned her horse down a wide street, paved with stones like many of the others in the capital.

I hadn't realized I'd have to face the ruling council of our land, but it made sense. If I was to eventually take over for Aunt Gill, working for them, they'd want to meet me. That didn't mean I was eager to meet them.

CHAPTER 3.

My aunt lived in an apartment in a tall building not far from the center of Willoughby. The door from the street led to a huge hall with a polished stone floor and white painted walls. Several doors led off the hall. Aunt Gill led me to the one with the number six on it and used a key to gain access. Inside, the three rooms on the ground floor included a kitchen, and dining and sitting rooms, both filled with ornate wooden and upholstered furniture. "The bedrooms are upstairs." Aunt Gill pointed to a straight stairway in the hall between the dining and sitting rooms. "Sweetheart, people here live a very different life from the one you're used to, but at least most of it will be recognizable to you. It is the places you'll go through the portals that will surprise you."

"Yes, I guess that's what I'm afraid of."

"There's no reason to be afraid. I'll make sure you're prepared for any eventuality. After I take you to the council tomorrow, we'll visit Morgan Fleming."

"You mentioned him before. Or her."

She grinned. "Oh, Morgan's definitely a man. He trained me, and Clare as well. He'll help prepare you for anything you might find."

"What about Cass?" They'd mentioned that name, too.

Aunt Gill nodded. "Eventually you'll be ready for what Cass can teach you. His expertise is quite different from Morgan's." She started for the stairs. "Right now, let's get you settled in your room."

I followed her up, carrying my bag and holding on to the handrail. I wasn't used to such a steep stairway. The small landing had three doors off it. Aunt Gill opened the one on the right and ushered me inside a room similar to mine back home. A single bed covered in a handmade quilt, a small table with a lamp, and a chest of drawers with a mirror hanging on the wall above it.

"I think you'll be comfortable here."

"Oh, very!" The familiarity of the room eased some of my nervousness.

"The door at the back of the landing leads to a bathroom with a sink, tub and toilet. I used some of what I've brought back from my travels to make it quite functional, if not fancy. You can wash up and change out of your traveling clothes in there."

I nodded. I did feel grimy after riding most of the

day, and my dust-covered skirt and blouse smelled less fresh than when I donned them in the morning.

"When you're finished, come back downstairs and we'll see whether there's anything in the kitchen we can eat for dinner." Her hand grabbed the door knob before she turned and came back. "If you don't know how something works in the bathroom just call, and I'll come in to show you."

I couldn't imagine what she meant until I entered the small room and looked around. Instead of the pump we had at home, there were knobs behind the sink, just like in the kitchen at Clare and Piers'. But what had me stumped was the tub, huge and deep, and with a few knobs like the sink. I looked forward to soaking in it, if I could figure out how to fill it. And the toilet looked nothing like the one in the outhouse back home, but it was clearly a toilet with a round seat and a box-shaped contraption above with a chain hanging down.

For now, I only washed my hands and face at the sink. I would have to ask my aunt how everything worked. When I traded my traveling clothes for a clean skirt and blouse, I wondered briefly what kinds of clothing my aunt would buy for me. She had to know what would be correct for the travels I might take.

I checked my face in the mirror in the bedroom. My blond hair was a little unkempt, but otherwise I looked the same as always, light blue eyes, an oval face and a straight nose. Why had Piers thought I looked like Gill? She had a beautiful face and golden hair. I patted my own hair into place. Satisfied with how I looked, I descended the staircase and went to look for my aunt in the kitchen. "We still have the food your mother sent. Perhaps I'll make some soup with the carrots and apples and we'll have it with some of the bread."

We'd fed apples to the horses, but there were plenty left. "That sounds good."

The corner cooking hearth was not unlike ours but much smaller. The kitchen was more like Clare's. As we ate our light supper, my aunt told me more about some of her travels. Now that I knew the reason for them, I could believe many of the destinations weren't on our world.

The soup was savory, even without any meat. The crunch of the carrots made it more filling. My aunt was a better cook than I expected. I finished my last spoonful and sat back in my chair. "No wonder I never heard of some of the lands you visited until you told us where you'd been."

"You'll go to these and other places." She pushed her empty bowl from her.

I nodded, my chest tightening with the strange mixture of excitement and trepidation I was becoming used to.

"Right now, we've both had a long day. We should make it an early night. Tomorrow will be even busier."

When I woke the next morning, it took a minute or two to realize I was at Gill's. As I untangled myself from the comforter and sheets, my aunt knocked on my door.

"Come in."

"I've brought you one of my dresses. It may be a little large on you, but will be much more appropriate for our meeting with the council than any of your clothing."

Aunt Gill had a fuller figure than I did, although we were about the same height. The dark blue dress reached my calves and had buttons running down the front and a slim skirt. "Thank you. How will we know what kind of clothing I'll need for the place we're going first?"

"There are certain styles that would be suitable wherever we go." She started to leave, then turned her head. "Shall I draw you a bath?"

"Oh, that would be wonderful!" She'd shown me how to operate the toilet the night before, but I'd been too tired then to learn more.

I took the dress and some undergarments to the bathroom where Aunt Gill was filling the tub with hot water from the spigot in the wall using the knobs to adjust the temperature. She handed me a bar of soap and a towel, then withdrew so I might bathe and dress.

The water was warm, but not hot and the soap smelled of lavender. My body relaxed as I scrubbed myself. But soon the water cooled and I got out, wiping off the droplets with the soft white towel. I dressed quickly and descended the stairs as my stomach rumbled with hunger.

We shared a quick breakfast of bread, cheese and tea, and then set out for one of the multistory brick buildings in the center of the city. My shoulders tensed. Aunt Gill hadn't told me much about the council or its members.

We entered the building and walked across a large hall with a high ceiling and an even shinier floor than the hall in Gill's building. She pushed open the door to a room on the right. The ruling council, consisting of five men and one woman, sat at a raised table at one end of the cavernous and dimly lit room. Dressed formally in dark suits, they looked very serious, stern and forbidding.

"Gillian, we're pleased you could join us today." An older man with snow white hair and keen dark eyes in a clean-shaven face rose from the center seat when we entered. "This must be your niece. Welcome, Anabet. I am Councilman Angus McClure." He bowed slightly.

"Sir." I wasn't sure whether I should bow or curtsy, so I just stood before him, waiting for him to go on.

"We have a rather delicate situation. Liam, please explain what has happened." He turned to the younger blond man on his left.

"The key to a newly-found portal was stolen before we could find out where it led. The person who took it used it to pass through the portal. We need you to follow the thief and bring back both him and the key."

"But how can we follow if he took the key?" I blurted.

"You'll have to ask Cass Holden to make another. Here are the necessary instructions." Angus held out a large envelope, and Gillian took it without a word.

I looked at my aunt. The more I heard about this Cass, the more intrigued I was.

"Do we know who stole the key?" Aunt Gill asked.

"We suspect it was Rolf Peters, but we can't be certain until you find him," Angus said.

"Why would Rolf steal it?" Gill asked.

Angus shook his head. "I'm afraid we don't know."

"He's working for Orson! I'm sure of it!" a slim man with dark hair and beard shouted.

"That's possible, Philip." Angus said with a brief nod.

"I'll take Bet to Morgan Fleming this morning to begin her defensive training. We'll go to Cass directly afterward."

"The sooner you follow the thief through the portal, the better," Angus said.

"Do we know anything about where this portal leads?" Aunt Gill asked.

Liam shook his head. "Since it was only recently discovered, no one has ever passed through it."

"It may or may not be a world with a highly

advanced technology," the woman council member said. "If it's a populous land, it will be difficult to find our thief."

"I'm sure Cass will be able to devise something that will help you find him and the key," Liam said.

"The important thing is to leave tomorrow or even sooner," Angus added.

"We won't fail in this assignment." Aunt Gill stood very straight, then looked at me. "Let's go, Bet. We need to prepare you. The quicker we start, the more we can do before   we   leave."

CHAPTER 4.

We left the building and walked down a cobblestone street filled with horse-drawn carts and pedestrians. I didn't know where to begin with my many questions, so I kept silent. I wanted to examine the shops along the way, but my aunt walked quickly past all of them. She turned a corner and I saw a most wondrous house. Surrounded by the ubiquitous tall brick buildings, it was only one story with a portico across the front curving around both sides. Two rounded white columns reached from the ground to the pitched roof. Three steps led up to the porch and massive wooden door.

Before Aunt Gill could knock, a man of medium height opened the door. His light brown hair was brushed back, but a lock fell across an open face that held a hint of a smile. His pants, shirt and vest were nondescript browns.

"You're early." He opened the door wider to allow us to enter.

Aunt Gill stepped over the threshold. "Time is of the essence."

"Isn't it always." His smile widened.

My aunt continued walking toward the back of the house. "Someone has stolen a portal key, and Bet and I must leave tomorrow to find and retrieve it." She spoke without preamble.

He finally closed the front door. "Tomorrow? I thought I'd have at least a week to work with your niece!" His shoulders slumped. "Ah, well, I guess we'll have to do what we can in the time we have." He bowed to me. "Welcome to my home, Bet. I'm Morgan Fleming. I'm sure before the day is out you'll wish you'd never heard of me."

He was a little older than I'd thought at first, perhaps my parents' age. "I hope you won't be sorry you heard of me," I said.

He chuckled. "She has your sense of humor, Gill. And your beauty. All right, first things first, establishing what skills you have. Can I assume you can use a knife?"

"You mean to cut things?" I made a slicing motion.

He ushered us through a door to the right. "That's a start. Come into the training room and we'll see how strong and agile you are."

The large training room had a high ceiling. A couple of tables held what appeared to be several weapons. Mats covered sections of the floor, but elsewhere many years of use had scuffed and scratched the wooden slats.

Morgan handed me a short knife with an intricately carved handle.

"Hold the handle here to use it as a weapon." He placed my fingers for me.

I followed his instruction and he nodded.

"Now, if you want to throw it, change the position of your fingers." He took the knife from me and showed me the different ways it could be held, had me try each one until he was satisfied.

Over the next two hours, he instructed me on how to defend myself, first with the knife, and then with my hands, legs and other parts of my body. How to fight off a larger, stronger man. How shifting my weight can be a kind of weapon. He was a stern taskmaster, exact in his instructions and movements, and he never smiled, not even when I succeeded in fending off his attempts to toss me to the mat. Through it all, I felt Aunt Gill studying me intently.

After a time, my arms felt bruised. My muscles ached, yet a sense of accomplishment filled me.

"You've done enough for now." Morgan stepped away from me and finally smiled. "All those years doing farm work built muscles and an agility that should help you. I suppose you've fought with animals that had their own minds." He patted his flat stomach. "I seem to have worked up an appetite. Will you ladies join me for lunch?"

I brushed my sweat-dampened hair off my

forehead and held out his knife.

He shook his head. "Keep it. It will serve you well. I no longer have a need for it, obliged to stay here and train younger, and more beautiful couriers." He had good manners, but I wondered why he no longer traveled. Had he reached an age where it was discouraged?

"Ladies first." His hand indicated a small sink in a corner of the room I hadn't noticed before. I washed my hands and face and dried them with a soft cloth.

He led the way to a large kitchen with a table and four chairs in the center and cabinets along every wall. Then he did the most extraordinary thing. He snapped his fingers and a fire lit beneath the open top of one of the cabinets. My eyes widened. Placing a grate over the fire, he used it like a hearth. He filled a kettle with water from a sink like the one I'd seen at my aunt's place and at Clare's. He put the kettle on the grate, then turned to us.

"Do you like shrimp?" he asked me.

"Shrimp?" I looked at my aunt for clarification.

She smiled at my confusion. "They're creatures that inhabit some seas. The meat inside the shell is sweet and tender, and especially delicious when seasoned properly."

"Oh, I'm willing to give that a try." I remembered the delicious shellfish Gill brought us once.

Morgan smiled, too. He was almost handsome when he did. Then he hummed a tune I didn't know and walked to a tall cupboard in the corner of the kitchen. When he opened it, a wave of cold flowed out, and I saw food inside. He removed a bowl filled with small C-shaped pink pieces. He noticed my astonishment and said, "Just a little something I brought back from my travels."

He put a shallow pan on the grate next to the kettle and added some butter. While it melted, he sprinkled a powder over the shrimp. I couldn't tell what it was until he added them to the pan and a strong, familiar aroma assailed my nose. "Pity I didn't have any garlic cloves but this powder will do. Gillian, be a dear and prepare a salad, would you?"

"It would be my humble pleasure." A smile curved her lips.

"Oh, and there should be a lemon in the chiller as well."

Aunt Gill took some greens and vegetables from the tall cabinet and tossed a lemon to Morgan. He caught it deftly with his left hand, promptly sliced it in two, and squeezed both halves over the cooking shrimp. The aroma intensified with the addition.

I helped my aunt put together a salad, slicing carrots and cucumbers. Morgan's shrimp were cooked by the time we finished, and we sat down to our meal.

I bit into a shrimp and my mouth cheered. "These are as good as you said." Firmer than chicken, almost chewy, the garlic and lemon juice strangely made the meat taste sweet. "What seas do these come from?"

"There are three lands I've traveled to where the shrimp are a staple food along the warm coastal waters," Aunt Gill replied.

"I've seen them cooked even more ways than we cook chicken and beef," Morgan added. He ate with gusto, enjoying his own cooking, frequently wiping his mouth with a serviette.

"I'll have to try some cooked other ways." Then I pursed my lips, thinking I'd been too forward, asking him to cook for me again. The salad vegetables were fresh, although I hadn't seen any gardens in Willoughby. "And the vegetables?"

"I grow them out back," Morgan said with a casual wave.

I was tempted to ask to see his vegetable patch. "So you're a gardener and cook as well as a defense teacher?" Was he also something of a wizard? I wasn't about to ask.

"Among other things. I'm glad you're enjoying your lunch."

I nodded. "Yes, I am. Thank you for everything."

My aunt swallowed some salad. "But I'm afraid that, once we've eaten, I'll have to take Bet to Cass Holden and see whether he can manage a key to the portal Rolf used."

"Are you sure Rolf took the real one?" I asked.

She frowned. "It hardly matters. We still must find the thief before he does any damage."

After thanking Morgan once more, we took our leave, and walked out into the sunlit street. As we made our way through the city, I thought about my questions again. I asked the one that had bothered me the most. "Aunt Gill, why is it so imperative to go after the man who stole the portal key? If Cass can make another, why does the council need the original?"

"Oh, no, it's not so much to bring back the key, although that's part of our mission. We don't want the key to fall into the wrong hands, and we have to prevent the thief from doing anything that will make it impossible to establish diplomatic relations with the land on the other side. He might steal something of importance and bring it back here."

"That seems to be a good part of your job." As I said it, a strange look crossed her face. "I mean, to make contact with the people at the other end of the portals."

"Well, yes, most of the time. Sometimes they're eager to meet us, to know there are other worlds. But occasionally we need to use diplomacy, tact or even guile to convince them. And other times, we observe without telling them anything."

"You said you mainly acted as a courier to bring documents or messages back and forth, right? And that's what I'll be doing?"

"Not just documents."

I stopped in my tracks and stared at her, as all the pieces fell into place. "You bring back...things, too, don't you? Sometimes without the knowledge of the owners. You keep those items to yourselves, like Morgan brought back the chiller, although how one man could do that I don't know. And you brought all those things in your bathroom. You don't even share what you've found with others here." I swallowed the bile filling my mouth. "You obtain those things by theft so how can you judge what Rolf Peters did?" My voice had risen. My lips trembled as I whispered, "Why didn't you tell me?"

"It isn't theft. Not exactly." She waved a hand. "In fact, most of the time, we're given what we bring back." She stopped and glared at me. "And if I HAD told you? Would you still have come to Willoughby with me?"

"Definitely not! Aunt Gillian, I won't do it!" I folded my arms across my chest defiantly. "In fact, take me back to your place so I might collect my things and return home!"

"Oh, Bet. Don't be so impetuous!" She sighed heavily, crossing her own arms.

"Impetuous? How can you say that? I won't resort to thievery of any sort and that's final!"

She studied my face but I couldn't read her expression. "Before you make a hasty decision, come with me on this mission. I can assure you, we won't engage in any activities you might find distasteful. Afterward you can decide whether you wish to continue to serve the council."

I frowned at her. Yes, I was curious now about what it was like to cross the portals to other lands, and to see how different they were. Blame it on my youth, or perhaps my thirst for knowledge. Reluctantly I continued on with my aunt to our next stop.

CHAPTER 5.

Morgan's strange house was nothing compared to the...hut that Cass Holden lived in. You couldn't call it anything else, with its thatched roof, irregularly-shaped door, mismatched windows, and crooked chimney. On the other hand, the man who answered the door when Aunt Gill rapped on it, was small, compact, and very neatly dressed in a brocade coat and heavy wool trousers.

"Gillian, my dear!" He took her hands in his small, gnarled ones and pulled her inside, then reached out for me. "And you must be Bet. Come in!" His deep voice befitted a much larger man.

My mouth fell open as I looked around inside. Open books, glassware containing liquids in a myriad of colors, a couple of maps, writing implements, and mugs holding what looked like the dregs of tea sat on a large, round table in the center of the single room. Similar items filled the seats of several mismatched chairs. Cass hurriedly swept the books off two armchairs and onto the floor. "Please sit. Have you had any lunch?"

"Morgan fed us," Aunt Gill said.

"Ah, Morgan." His eyes focused inward as if he was thinking that over. Finally, he sighed. "Well, what brings you to my modest dwelling?" His grin had returned.

My aunt sat and steepled her fingers in front of her. "The council sent us. Someone has stolen the key to a newly found portal and fled there with it. The council thinks it was Rolf Peters. They're unclear about his intentions, but we've been asked to bring back both the thief and the key."

"Hmm. That could be a problem." Cass stroked his short black beard that didn't match his wispy blond hair.

Aunt Gill nodded. "Yes, that's what they said."

Cass sighed. "I assume they want me to conjure up another key to use to go after him. Do we know what's on the other side of the portal?"

"Liam thinks it's a more advanced civilization. I presume he means a mechanized society. Self-propelled vehicles and devices that wash clothes." She frowned. "Machines that won't work here, unfortunately, because we don't have the means to power them."

"Electricity. Hmm." He scratched his head. "I'll have to think about what kind of key you'll need. It might have to be substantial."

"Why?" I blurted. "Isn't a key just a key, made to fit

in a lock and open a door?" Then I recalled Aunt Gill said everyday objects could be 'keys'. "Why would this one have to be more substantial?"

"The more progressive a society, the more intricate the portal to it. The key would have to address all of those intricacies," Cass explained.

"Oh!"

"I don't suppose you've ever seen a portal key." He narrowed his eyes as he looked at me over his spectacles.

"Only a proper door key." I didn't dare ask where the keys usually came from.

He laughed, and Aunt Gill joined him. "She has a lot to learn, doesn't she?" he asked.

"And not much time to learn it, I'm afraid," Aunt Gill said.

I remembered my dream again. "Perhaps you can use a seashell."

"Perhaps, but only if you're going to an island. Well, down to business. Where is this portal?" Cass asked.

Aunt Gill handed him the envelope Councilman Liam had given her. "I believe this is all the council knows."

Cass removed a flimsy sheet of paper. I couldn't see the writing on it, but perhaps I couldn't have read it if I had. He chuckled. "Well, well. This new portal is down by the docks. Do you know the statue of General Mundson?"

"The one where the sculptor paid more attention to the details of the horse's rump and tail than to the general?" Aunt Gill asked.

"Yes. That's the one. You must pass between the legs of the horse." He stopped as his eyes studied the page.

"But which way? From which side, I mean?" I pictured the statue in my mind although I'd never seen it. A horse is a horse, after all.

"Now let me see." Cass consulted the paper, holding it in his right hand and waving his left in a circle. "Yes, I see. With the horse's head on your left, you bend a bit to proceed under the horse near the stirrups."

"Won't it look odd to anyone around?" How could my aunt and I do this unobtrusively?

Aunt Gill nodded. "There are always children playing around the statue. That might pose an additional problem for us."

"Especially since I'm not a child and neither are you, Aunt Gill." I was new to all of this, but something Aunt Gill said earlier sparked an idea. "We could drop something and pretend to look for it, something that would roll under the horse."

"There's always the danger someone else will pick it up first," she argued. "But we can keep that in mind."

"Oh." I frowned. It seemed my suggestions so far hadn't helped. "And I suppose the key would have to be large to be substantial."

"Not necessarily," Cass said. "I know just the thing.

An apple. Yes, and I can imbue it with other properties. Why, it might also serve to lead you to the thief and the original key. Hmmm." He stroked his beard again. Then he rummaged through one of the books, but soon dropped it, picklng up another.

"How could it do that?" I still had so many questions.

"Hmm?" Cass seemed surprised to see us still there, but then he smiled at me. "Once you're on the other side, if you bite into it, you'll be able to find anything that doesn't belong in that world."

"Like Rolf and the key!" Aunt Gill clapped her hands. "Oh, that's marvelous."

"Well, I'd best be getting to it," Cass said. "I'm sure you ladies have preparations to make." He went back to his book.

"Yes we do." Aunt Gill stood. "Come, Bet. We should see to your travel wardrobe."

We left the strange house and its even stranger occupant, walking back toward one of the major streets. This time we walked slowly enough that I could look into the windows of the shops. The variety of merchandise was overwhelming: household items, such as pots and dishware, clothing for men, women, and children, and foodstuffs, even a bookstore and one selling horse bridles.

I followed my aunt into a store called Elegance. It wasn't large, but every inch was filled with brightly-colored dresses. I'd never seen so many. Now I knew where Aunt Gill purchased the garments she favored. Several shelves held matching shoes, some with heels so high I couldn't imagine walking in them. A sweet, flowery scent preceded a short woman with bright red hair who walked towards us, smiled broadly and spread her arms wide. "Gillian! So good to see you again."

Aunt Gill hugged her, then stepped back. "Fiona, this is my niece, Anabet. We need some dresses for her."

"Will you be traveling with your aunt?" Fiona asked, looking me over. But she didn't wait for me to reply. "I'm sure I have just the thing! Gill, remember the book Clare brought back? The one from a world where the women were in charge of everything?" Her brow creased. "I don't think it was written there but in another world all together."

Aunt Gill's forehead creased. "No, I don't recall it."

"It was about a farm girl who traveled to the city and fell in love with a member of the royal family. Later she decided that city ways were not to her liking. Now, what was it called?" She shook the curls framing her head. "Oh, it doesn't really matter. The important thing is the dress the Duke bought for her to wear to a ball, and I made one based on the description in the book."

She disappeared into the back of the shop, but soon returned carrying a frock in a light gray, smooth fabric. It was more elaborate than the outfit I was wearing, with a high, stiff white collar, and silvery buttons from the neckline to the waist, short and puffy sleeves, and a skirt that looked like it would only reach my knees. It was much more ornate than anything I had ever worn before. "Try this on." Fiona held it out to me.

She took me to a small alcove with a cloth curtain across it so I could change into the dress. As I put it on, I recalled my dream and how I felt out of place because my plain clothes. This would have been much more appropriate at that dinner. When I returned, I watched my aunt's face. She beamed.

"Isn't she lovely in it?" Fiona asked.

I dared to look at myself in Fiona's mirror. The dress made me look beautiful and made my hair look almost golden. Like Gill's. "But will this be appropriate in the place we're going?" I had no idea what they wore in 'advanced civilizations' if the world at the other end of the portal was one.

"It's not as intricate as the clothes they wore in the only place I've been with the kind of technology we believe they have." Aunt Gill examined the fabric. "But this will do nicely."

Over the next half hour, I tried on a dozen outfits and my aunt chose two. One was another dress, much simpler than the gray one. It was pale green with a round neck. I wondered how I could get into it, but found out when I tried it on. A fastener up the middle of the back that Aunt Gill called a zip. The dark blue skirt and blouse she said would be unremarkable anywhere I went so I could blend in appeared very similar to my own clothes, but I didn't argue. My aunt paid Fiona and said she would see her again soon.

As we left the dress shop with my packages, I asked, "Where are we going now?"

"We should go back to Morgan's. There's still so much for him to teach you and we still have some time today."

We returned to Morgan's house. Aunt Gill knocked on the door, but received no answer. Peering in the front window, I didn't see any movement inside. Nothing looked disturbed, except Morgan was gone.

"Perhaps he's gone somewhere," I suggested. "He doesn't stay here all the time, does he?"

"He expected we might return. He couldn't have gone far." Her eyes narrowed and a crease appeared between them.

"Should we look in his back garden?"

My aunt smiled. "That's a good idea." I followed her around the house to the small square yard filled with neat rows of herbs and vegetables, but saw no sign of Morgan.

We returned to the front door and knocked again, this time a little harder. The door swung open. Without hesitation, Aunt Gill stepped inside and called out,

"Morgan! Where are you?"

We walked into the kitchen where we'd eaten with him only a few hours earlier. A teapot and a half-full cup sat on the table next to a plate of biscuits, one with a bite taken out of it.

"He must have been in the middle of his afternoon tea when he left," I surmised, touching the still-hot pot.

"Something's wrong." Aunt Gill's forehead creased again and she frowned. "We must return to the council at once and let them know!"

CHAPTER 6.

Gill and I hurried back to the large brick building. We raced so quickly that my voice caught. "Morgan's disappearance is unusual, isn't it? He didn't go out for a stroll somewhere?"

My aunt didn't answer. We entered the building and opened the doors to a darkened council chamber with no signs of the council members. "Most peculiar." Gill approached the dais and the empty table and chairs.

"What do we do now?" I remained near the doorway. "Where do the council members go when they aren't meeting?"

A rustle came from behind the table, and the only female council member stood from where she'd been crouching. "Gillian! Thank the Goddess it's you! I was afraid someone would see me."

"What's happened?" Aunt Gill continued toward her. "Where are the others?"

"As you know, Orson's faction have argued over

the way we send travelers through the portals. Well, I'm afraid it's progressed much further than protests and complaints. Liam, Angus and Philip had to move operations to the safe house. When you arrived I was gathering the papers we'll need."

"Leone, Morgan's missing." Aunt Gillian's voice quavered slightly.

The woman's shoulders slumped. "Oh, no! We hoped he could help us."

Color drained from my aunt's face. "Could Orson have taken him?"

"I hope not. We cannot let Orson take control, and if he has Morgan, he has an advantage. Ever since the first time he traveled, Orson has been intent on bringing back technology to destroy the balance of power here on Nokar."

I wondered what issues Orson had with the council, but didn't dare ask. "Do you think Orson had anything to do with the theft of the portal key?"

Leone nodded. "It seems likely. We've speculated that Orson sent Rolf to find weapons we know nothing about." She pressed her lips together, then released her breath. "Gillian, with Morgan gone, I'm afraid you'll have to help us find Orson and his minions."

"Of course. But what about the journey you needed me to take with Bet? If your speculations are correct who will go after Rolf and stop him from bringing

Orson new weapons?"

Leone studied me a moment. "Bet will have to go alone, I'm afraid. It's as important to find Rolf as it is to find Orson."

"But I'm not ready!" My heart thudded. "I've only had brief training with Morgan. Aunt Gill, please tell her I can't do this alone!" My plea became a whine. "You promised to come with me on my first journey." I was crying by then.

My aunt put her hands on my shoulders and squeezed. "You'll have to go by yourself, my dear. You're not really alone. Go back to Cass and let him know what's happening. He'll guide you to the portal and give you all you'll need to accomplish your task. All you have to do is go through the portal, find the thief and key, and return."

"What if Cass is gone too, like Morgan?" Hot tears filled my eyes.

"Do you know your way to your aunt's home?" Leone asked.

I nodded and swallowed the bile that filled my mouth.

"Whether or not Cass is there, return to Gillian's apartment for anything you need. We'll have someone watching to see whether Cass returns with you." Leone pressed her lips together, then popped them open. "Don't worry child. Just do as you're told."

"You can do this, Bet. We wouldn't send you if we

didn't think so. We're counting on you." Aunt Gill squeezed my shoulder again, but I wasn't as certain as she was.

They hurried to the paneled wall behind the council desk. Leone pressed a medallion in the center of a panel. Part of the wall slid open, Gill glanced back with pursed lips, and then they slipped through. Alone in the huge council chamber, my hands shook with my self-doubt. Perhaps if my instructions came from my aunt, I'd feel more comfortable with them, but I knew I had to follow them no matter who issued the orders.

I walked on rubbery legs from the building into the bright sunshine. People passed by as if nothing unusual had happened. I thought I knew the way back to Cass' strange place. I must have taken a wrong turn, because I found myself in an unfamiliar part of the city with many smaller houses. My throat tightened and my hands began to sweat. "You can do this, Bet," I told myself as I retraced my steps. "It can't be far." Finally I saw a tall, thin tower I remembered from earlier in the day. Soon after, I found Cass' house again and knocked on his door, hoping he was still where he should be.

"Coming, coming," he called. His footsteps grew louder. "Bet! Back so soon? Where's your aunt?" He looked past me and frowned.

"Oh, Cass, there's been some trouble. Morgan's missing, and someone named Orson is planning a coup, and the council has gone into hiding and taken Aunt Gill with them, and..." The words tumbled out of my mouth.

Cass reached out one of his gnarled hands and grasped my arm, pulling me inside. "There, there. Why don't you come sit down and tell old Cass all about it."

I sat in an unexpectedly dainty chair and tried to slow my breathing. I still clutched the bags from the clothing shop, so I put them down gently. "Morgan is gone. Aunt Gill and Leone left me alone in the council room." I looked up into his caring eyes. "They said you would help me to carry out the mission, but how can I do it alone? I'm still not trained, not ready. I have no idea what to do to find Rolf."

"Oh, dear! Well, I guess it can't be helped." He forced a smile. "At least you'll be happy to know I'm almost finished." He left for a moment and returned holding a drawstring bag. He put the contents of the bag, three red apples and one green, on a small round table next to my chair. He held out the green one. "This will be your portal key. Most people prefer red apples, so it should be safe from any thief. It will enable you to pass under the horse and through the threshold to the other world. You'll use it again to return to the same spot."

He put the new portal key on the table and picked up one of the others. "One bite of any of these will allow you to find anything that's lost, take you to anything in the other world that doesn't belong there." He studied my face. "Do you understand?"

"Yes. I mean, I think so. The red apples will help me find Rolf and the key he stole after I use the green one to go through the portal." I watched his face to see whether I got it right.

"Very good." He put the red apples back into the bag and handed it to me. "I'm afraid I can't help you with any other preparations."

My knees shook, but I knew I had to go on alone. "Aunt Gill bought me some clothes. I should change into one of the dresses before I leave. Oh, and one more thing. I'm to return to her place with you so the council will know you've done your part."

"So that's what we must do. As soon as I finish with this other apple." He held the green one high in one hand, said a few words in an unknown language. He waved his other hand over it, and said a few different words.

"Now, what about money? Did Gillian give you any?"

"No, but I have these coins from my father."

Cass looked them over. "There's not much here to work with I'm afraid, but you'll need currency wherever you go." He did some more mumbo-jumbo, and the coins became a small stack of paper with a distinct glow to it. "This will become whatever is used where you're going."

After fifteen minutes, he had finished. He gave me the glowing paper and put the green apple key into the bag with the others. "After you, my dear." He ushered me out, following close behind, and locked his door with a hand signal.

Cass came with me to Aunt Gill's place. But when we reached her door and I turned the knob, it was locked.

"Not to worry," Cass said, waving a hand clockwise, then counterclockwise over the lock. The door clicked open.

My eyes opened wide. "Could I learn to do that?" I knew the answer even before he shook his head. I wasn't a wizard, or magician, or whatever he called himself.

It was eerily quiet inside, even quieter than at Morgan's place. I quickly changed into the beautiful new gray dress. I packed the rest in the carry-all I'd used to bring my things from home. At the last minute, I added one of my own outfits and my nightdress, comb and toothbrush. Ready as possible, I returned to Cass, who waited patiently in the entryway.

"Has anyone from the council come?" I didn't see anyone.

"No, but no matter."

My heart beat wildly. If I felt like this in the relative safety of Aunt Gillian's home, how would I feel when I crossed over to the unknown of the world?

"I'm ready." I could hear the trepidation in my voice.

"You're better off being nervous than too

confident." He patted my shoulder. "Come. We need to reach the portal in daylight." We walked side by side.

I stopped in my tracks. "Why?" It hadn't occurred to me before that there would be any time limit.

"You don't want to fetch up in a strange place in the dark, do you? We've found that often the time of day is approximately the same on both sides of the portals." He urged me onward. "Not always the same year or time of year, but the same hour."

"Oh!" I seemed to be saying that word a lot, but what he said made sense.

We walked through a part of the town I'd never seen before. The buildings were smaller than in the center of the city and in need of paint. It was shabbier than the places where Morgan and Cass lived. I caught the salty scent of the sea after a while and then a glimpse of the tall white sails of many ships. We reached the semi-circular harbor. A paved, open area lay close to the seawall. In the center stood the largest statue I'd ever seen, a mounted soldier brandishing a sword.

My heart sank as I looked at the statue. It crawled with children from toddlers to ten- or twelve-year-olds, running and scrambling under the horse's legs.

"How will I ever approach the statue without being seen?" We'd discussed this before, of course, but hadn't formed a plan. I'd expected to have Aunt Gill with me to lead the way.

"We have a little time." Cass' gaze swept over the young ones and adults in the area, then looked out to sea and the sun, still above the horizon, but not by much.

I approached the statue. My heart beat so hard my breath came in gasps. Too many people filled the area to even consider the idea of dropping something under the horse and bending to pick it up so I could pass through the portal.

"Let's go, children," a woman, wearing a red cape over her dark gray suit, called. Reluctantly, one-by-one, they abandoned the statue and formed two long lines in front of her. After she'd counted heads and nodded in satisfaction, she turned and led them away. A few adults and children remained around General Mundson and his horse, but far fewer than before.

I looked at Cass and he nodded. I pretended to examine the horse and moved ever closer to the legs. I saw my chance, and clutching the bag of apples in one hand, and the carry-all in the other, I bent slightly to make my way through the portal...

For a moment, everything around me muted as I was enveloped in blinding light. All sound ceased as if my ears stopped working. Panic crushed my chest. Would I be in this limbo forever? Before fear could devour me, I was thrust into a noisy, smelly, confusing scene.

I don't know what disturbed me the most, the

cacophony of sounds, the noxious odors, the sight of buildings like trees that never stopped growing, extending as far as the eye could see in every direction, or the oppressive heat and crush of people, so many people. Maybe it was the monsters, moving across my line of vision from left to right, machines that had swallowed people but with no horses to draw them forward. Would they gobble me up too, along with my bag of apples? Maybe it was the faces of every color and dressed in an assortment of fabrics, all in one spot at the same time, the same spot as me.

My feet stood on an island, a raised piece of land, completely surrounded by this sea of folks. Nearby, enclosed by a very low fence to keep it from escaping, was a small square of grass with a tiny tree bravely growing in its center, battling the glass and metal for every ray of sunlight.

The people around me seemed to be waiting for something. Without warning, the conveyances ceased moving. The crowd flowed across in front of them, carrying me along with them. I walked as slowly as I could, trying to get my bearings, until an older woman said, "The sign means you should walk. You don't have much time." She pointed to a green stick figure of someone walking. As I tread faster, numbers appeared, counting down from twenty. Was it some sort of magic?

When I finally arrived at the other side of the road

and stepped up, the numbers were replaced by a red hand. I stopped to catch my breath, then thought it prudent to move out of the path of the people rushing by like a horse with blinders on. I reached the glass wall of the nearest building and leaned against it, observing the scene before me through wide open eyes. Where was I? What manner of place was this?

CHAPTER 7.

As I pressed up against the smooth wall of an impossibly tall building, people rushed past without seeing me until a woman stopped.

"You'd better move along if you don't want to be trampled." She grimaced as she looked me up and down, then moved on.

My eyes pooled. How could I carry out my task in this strange place? No one told me it would be this way.

Another woman, this one younger, perhaps my age, stopped and stared. "Are you all right? Lost?"

"What?" I sighed. We seemed to speak the same language even though her pronunciation was so different. Was the little I understood of her speech an artifact of passing through a portal? No one mentioned that either. "I've had a long day, a long journey. I...I need to rest a moment."

She nodded. "I understand."

How could she understand? She belonged here,

dressed in the dark-blue pants many of the citizens of this place wore, with a strange shirt with no buttons but an image of someone feeding an apple to a horse across her ample chest. The animal looked like those we had at home, so maybe it wasn't so different here. Her shoes were even odder than her clothes, made of fabric rather than leather, with stripes of red and green, and laces like the brogues I wore when the ground was muddy. She wore her reddish-brown hair pulled up in a tail like a horse's, long and thick, hanging down her back.

Her gaze swept over me and she squinted at my dress. "Are you from England? Or maybe Ireland?"

"What?" Those must be other lands of this world. "Oh, because of my speech."

"Yes, your accent too. And other things. Not that it matters, of course. I'm Carolyn." She held out a small hand, not too clean, with several broken nails.

I didn't want to appear unfriendly. Perhaps she could aid me. "I'm Anabet." I shook the proffered hand. "Most just call me 'Bet'."

"So, Bet." Carolyn indicated my carry-all. "Where are you going?"

"I need to find lodgings for tonight." I didn't know where to start.

"Well, then this is your lucky day. You can come with me to the why!" She grinned and put her arm through mine. "C'mon."

How could I refuse? I wondered, though, where she might be taking me. I didn't know what the 'why' might be, or even who she was or why she was helping me. I'd only find out by accompanying her. I would start my search for the thief and the portal key in the morning, and meanwhile learn about this strange place and the people who lived here. Then I could bring that knowledge back with me, too.

We walked along together on the raised areas near the buildings. The slightly lower black roadways allowed passage of the horseless carriages. I gnawed on questions I could ask that didn't divulge my origin, or my mission. "Have you always lived here?"

"No, I'm from the Midwest, Ohio."

Another city or country? "So why did you come here?" I took a stab at a possible reason. "For some kind of work?"

"Most people who come to New York come looking for a job. Didn't you?"

I hesitated, but didn't think it could hurt to reply vaguely. "I'm here to look for a countryman of mine."

She grinned. "Do you know where he's staying?"

"Unfortunately, no. But I have a way to find him." I squeezed the handle of the bag holding my apples.

"Well, you can start looking tomorrow. Tonight, you're coming with me!" She tugged with the hand through my arm and drew me along. We crossed a few of the lower roadways, and then suddenly, spread out before us, grass and trees as far as I could see, with not a single building marring the vista. She led me down a meandering walkway, filled with other people passing this way and that. I wanted to stop and look at them, but Carolyn wouldn't let me. Occasionally, we passed a slow-moving horse-drawn cart and I felt a desire to feed them, they were so emaciated. I was much more at home.

Citizens sat on benches along a walk that passed under other roadways. I could hear the rumble of the monster conveyances over my head, but Carolyn ignored them so I tried to. My eyes widened, taking in everything. Looking to each side, I could still see the huge buildings that lined the greenway.

Our path took us to an edge of the park and we crossed another roadway, away from its comforting familiarity. A short while later we came to a building not as tall as some with a sign over the door; it read 'YWCA'. I couldn't imagine how to pronounce those letters. No wonder Carolyn called it the Y.

It was cool inside the entry hall, large like the one in Aunt Gill's building. Several women looked at us as we entered, their eyes studying me and what I wore. Aunt Gill had been wrong about the clothing she'd bought me. The dress I had on didn't fit in here at all. I wondered if I'd have to find pants and shirts like everyone else wore. Then again, I wouldn't be in this strange land long enough for it to matter.

A woman with a slim figure and long blond hair, pulled back like Carolyn's, approached us. "Where'd you find this one, Caro?" she asked. "I bet your mother tired of you bringing home strays all the time." She, too, spoke the same language, but her voice sounded different from Carolyn's.

"No need to be nasty, Danni," Carolyn replied. "She just needs a place to crash tonight. She'll be safer here than anywhere else."

Another woman, with skin as dark as I imagined the island people Aunt Gill told us about, joined us. "She'll have to register." She turned to me and said very slowly, "Do you have any money?"

"Yes, of course!" I took out the pouch with the coins Father had given me and Cass had worked his magic on.

"Oh, look Willy. She speaks!" Danni said as if I wasn't there or couldn't hear or understand.

I took out the rectangles of papers and held them out, not knowing how much it was.

Willy laughed. "That's just about enough for one night."

"How'd you expect to pay for a room or any meals with that?" Danni rolled her eyes. "You'll have to look for a job if you want to stay here longer than that."

"I can take her." Carolyn held on to my arm in a

protective manner, propelling me away from the other two.

A woman with short and curly brown hair, older than the others, called me to a high table and handed me a piece of paper. "Fill this out. It's eighty dollars for the night." I handed over the money I had and she took most of it. "There's not enough left for a meal ticket. Sorry." She shrugged and didn't sound as if she meant it.

The paper asked for my name and other details. I didn't know what they all meant, but I wrote down what I could using the strange writing instrument the woman gave me, then returned them to the woman. "I'm sorry but there are some things I don't know."

"That's OK, dearie. You're not the first foreigner we've had here." She gave me another sheet. "These are the house rules. Obey 'em and you can stay as long as you like. Of course, it'll cost you more money. Caro, take her up to 717. She'll be sharing with Monique."

I took my belongings, including the sack of apples, and followed Carolyn to a door without a number on it, except for the half-circle above it with numbers from one to ten and an arrow moving slowly. When the indicator reached '1', the door slid to one side. I tried to keep my mouth from falling open as Carolyn ushered me through the doorway into a tiny room.

There were more numbers on one wall with a kind of knob next to each. As Carolyn pushed the one next to the number '7', the door swooshed closed and I felt the room rumble.

"You're up on seven," Carolyn said.

Were we actually ascending? Just as suddenly as it started, the motion of the little room stopped and the strange door slid open again. Outside was a dark and dingy hallway. We walked along it until Carolyn stopped in front of a door with '717' on it. By this time, I didn't know what to expect.

Carolyn knocked lightly on the wood and a petite woman with very short black hair and strangely-slanted dark eyes pulled it open.

"Monique, Shelley assigned Bet to your room," Carolyn told her.

"I knew I wouldn't have it to myself for long," Monique complained, but she was smiling. "Welcome to my little corner of the Y."

"Thank you." I entered the room and looked around. It was an ordinary bedroom with two narrow beds, a table, a chair and a clothing dresser. But then I looked closely at the things on the table. I couldn't begin to imagine what they were. The largest object was in two pieces, hinged together like a door on its side, with the upright part at right angles to the one flat on the desk. Next to it was a thin rectangular box about the size of a cake of soap, but it had a black frame around a piece of glass, and the last was a funny shape, gray and black with a little wheel stuck in the top.

Monique reached up a slim arm and patted my shoulder. "Don't worry, Caro. I'll take care of her."

"Well, I guess I'll see you both tomorrow." Carolyn left me with Monique and I didn't know what to say to her.

She pointed to the bed further from the small window. "That's yours."

I could have guessed it. The other one was strewn with bedclothes and garments. The young woman wasn't wearing the uniform I'd come to associate with everyone here. Instead of the blue pants and shirts with pictures, she wore black hose under a short, dark gray, loose dress. The clothing on her bed was all black or gray.

"Where may I put my things?" I asked her.

She glanced at my bag, walked to the dresser, opened a drawer to pull out the contents, and then crammed it all into another drawer that was already quite full. "You can have this one."

I nodded and smiled at her. "Thank you."

"You're very polite. British I take it."

Those were the last words she spoke to me as she turned to the table and began to tap her fingers on the flat part of the hinged device. Letters appeared on the upright part, then words. I didn't want to pry so I set to work, putting my things carefully in the drawer, but my mind whirled with all the new things I'd seen.

CHAPTER 8

I opened my eyes and snapped them shut. Where was I? I reopened them more slowly and looked around. The sight of Monique, asleep in the bed next to mine, the covers pulled up to her chin and her mouth partly open, reminded me of the events of the previous day. I stood quietly and tiptoed into the tiny bathroom, washed my hands and face with warm water and the sweet smelling soap Monique used, and sat on the odd toilet. Instead of the pull cord like the one at Aunt Gill's, it had a lever on the side to add water to the bowl and swirl it around before draining somehow. I removed my nightdress and put on my underthings and my skirt and blouse. These clothes seemed closer to what the people wore here than the dress I'd worn the day before.

"Bet, you're awake." Monique smiled when I returned to the bedroom, then her eyelids fell again. I took my drawstring bag and let myself out with as little noise as possible, then walked down the narrow hallway to what Carolyn had called the elevator, hoping I'd be able to operate it. I still felt strange being up so high and had avoided looking through the window in the room.

Two other women stood in front of the elevator door. As I approached, the door opened and I went through after them, allowing the taller one to push the button next to the number one. The feeling of motion was more noticeable this time, as if we were dropping too fast. I held my breath. Soon, the door opened on the large entryway, and I sighed with relief.

Out on the sunlit street, I took one of Cass' red apples from the bag. It would serve as my breakfast and hopefully lead me to the thief and the portal key he'd taken. I bit into the crisp red skin, chewing slowly, savoring the slightly tart flavor. This might be the only food I'd have for a while. Nothing happened right away. I continued walking, back towards the park Carolyn had taken me through. I didn't know how I'd find the spot where the portal had deposited me, but at that moment I had another objective.

I hadn't walked far before a bright beam of light appeared, leading in a straight line in front of me. No one else seemed to notice it. Cass had never explained how the apple would lead me to Rolf Peters. I should have asked. Was this it? I followed the beam down the walk lining the roadway opposite the park for a while. It turned abruptly to the left in front of some steps leading up to an impressive building with the words 'Museum of Natural

History' over the doors. The building wasn't as tall as most, but was very distinctive, with a monumental central tower, corner turrets capped by conical roofs and ringed with heraldic birds. The facade combined different rocks, some smooth with a warm, red tint. The entire thing was decorated with turrets, finials and towers like a castle in a book. I could have stood, staring at it for hours but there were more important things to do, and people rushing past me to enter.

I followed the beam of light into the building and then to a huge hall. It felt much cooler inside. High ceilings made the murmurs of many people echo. I didn't know what a 'museum' was and wished I could explore, but the beam of light persisted and led me down a corridor to another room, where it stopped. Several people strolled around and paused every once in a while to look at some very large rocks. Was one of the men Rolf? If not, why did the light bring me there?

I walked over to one of the rocks, hoping it would give me a clue. Engraved on a shiny metal square in front of it were the words:

The Willamette Meteorite is a rare and important scientific specimen that was found in the Willamette Valley of Oregon and acquired by the Museum in 1906. In structure it is a metallic iron meteorite, weighing over 15.5 tons, the largest meteorite ever found in the United

States, and the sixth largest meteorite in the world.

The words didn't tell me much. What could it have to do with Rolf, the key or the portals? The apple was still in my hand. I took another bite, hoping it would bring back the light, but it didn't. I chewed slowly, considering what to do next.

I looked at the other rocks and read about them. From what I could surmise, meteorites were found in many places on this world, but they were 'alien' to it, coming from a 'solar system' or 'galaxy'; sometimes one term was used and other times the other. At least I now knew why biting the apple brought me here. I might need another way to find Rolf. He and I weren't the only things that didn't belong in this city. Biting one of the apples could bring me to any of them.

With nothing else to help me in this building. I walked back the way I came, out into the hot street, and then stopped. Now what?

If Cass' apple didn't take me to Rolf, how would I ever find him? I looked this way and that, at the crowds, rushing who knew where. There had to be thousands of people in this city, and he could be anywhere.

All I could think of was to go back to the two places I knew: the spot where I arrived in this land, and the Y. I crossed the roadway to the park. At least there I felt more at home, not that it was anything like the farm, but it was green and I wasn't so hemmed in by the huge buildings. I began the long walk back to the Y on that side of the street.

This time, without the light beam to focus me, I took the time to look at my surroundings.

"There you are."

I turned at the familiar voice and saw Carolyn.

"You left this morning without saying 'good-bye', but I knew you had something to do. Any luck finding the guy you were looking for?"

"No. I thought he might be at the museum." I stretched the truth again. It was becoming easier and easier to dissemble. "But I didn't see him." If Cass' apples didn't work, what would I do? Then again, how would I know Rolf when or if I found him? Something else I should have asked before I was rushed to the portal.

Carolyn was still talking. "Well, I heard they're hiring at Satellite. Ever been a waitress?"

"In a restaurant, you mean?" I'd only been to restaurants a few times, and certainly never worked in one.

"Yes. Jobs like those don't pay well, I'll admit, but you can make it up in tips."

I still had difficulty understanding her. "Are you saying that if we work as waitresses we can earn money for food and I can pay for another night at the Y?" It seemed it would take me longer than I thought to find Rolf, so I had to be prepared. I couldn't go home until I accomplished my task.

"Yup. C'mon. It's not far." She linked her arm in mine and led me as she had the day before. This city was so confusing. I couldn't have found anything without her. After walking for about five minutes, Carolyn stopped in front of an older building, and opened a glass door. People sat at many of the tables inside and a thin young woman carried plates of food, weaved her way among them.

Carolyn asked her, "Where's the manager?"

With her hands full of plates, she used her head to indicate the back of the place. "Hal's in the back." We made our way there and met a short, bald man who reminded me of the mayor of Romik.

"Can I help you lovely ladies?" He smiled broadly.

Carolyn took the lead. "We understand you're hiring."

He looked us over. I wondered what he thought of my odd clothes. But based on where he was focused, I didn't think he was thinking about that. "Ever waited tables before?"

I looked at Carolyn and she answered for both of us. "Yes, of course."

"Okay, seven bucks an hour. I'm the manager, Hal Parker. I'll see how you do today and decide if I should keep you on."

"Eight bucks," Carolyn replied. "You know minimum wage is more than that!"

It seemed prudent to remain silent.

"Seven fifty and not a cent more."

Carolyn narrowed her eyes, then nodded. "Only if we get to keep our tips. Bet, let's get to work."

I'd have to watch my new friend carefully if I was going to do this job. It seemed simple, but likely wasn't.

Hal called to me. "You, Blondie, take tables one, two and three at the front and the first two booths."

I looked where he pointed and nodded. He handed me a bright green apron that said 'Satellite' across the front. I put it on, swallowed my misgivings, and went to one of my assigned tables where two women sat, perusing a rectangular card. They both looked up as I approached. I cleared my throat and said, "I'm your waitress."

"I'll have a strawberry daiquiri, and a chicken Caesar salad," one of them said immediately. She had blond hair like I did, but with purple streaks in it. Had it grown that way? "Aren't you going to write it down?"

"I believe I can remember a strawberry daiquiri." I stumbled a bit over the unfamiliar word. "And salad with chicken."

"That's a Caesar salad."

"Right." I turned to her companion and waited. The second woman had dark hair, almost black, and eyes a warm brown. Her skin was the color of a strong cup of tea.

"You're not from around here," she said. While I tried to decide how to reply, she went on. "How is the salmon today?"

I didn't know, of course. "I haven't tasted it, but I'm sure it's quite good."

She frowned. "I'll have a turkey and Swiss sandwich, and iced tea."

"Turkey and Swiss sandwich and iced tea," I repeated, then turned toward the swinging doors that the other waitress had brought the food from, hoping that was where it was prepared.

I walked into a huge kitchen. The counters were a silvery metal and there was an entire section similar to the stove in Morgan's kitchen. One of the people working there, wearing a white jacket and a net over his hair, caught sight of me. "Yes?"

"I need a salad with chicken. A Caesar salad that is. And a turkey and Swiss sandwich. A...a strawberry dickery and an iced tea."

"You one of the new waitresses?"

"Yes, I am. I'm Bet."

He nodded. "You heard the lady," he yelled to two others who were busy stirring the pots on the stove. "I'm Oscar, the sous chef. You can get the drinks from the bartender," he told me. "After you serve them, come back and the food will be ready. You did enter the orders on the computer, didn't you?"

I didn't know what he was talking about but had to say, "I will. Thank you." I smiled at him. "Um, where do I find the bartender?"

His brow creased. "Behind the bar," he said, pointing to the doors I'd just come through. He was shaking his head as he walked away.

"Yes, of course." I went back into the restaurant and saw what he meant. Along the opposite wall was an ornate bar, much like in the tavern in Romik. I approached and tried to get the attention of the man behind it.

He had curly, ginger hair and some strange markings on the parts of his arms revealed by his rolled up white shirt sleeves. When he finally saw me and came over I noticed he had the bluest eyes I'd ever seen.

"How can I help you?" His deep voice went with his large build.

"One of my customers wants a strawberry..." I suddenly couldn't remember the odd word she used.

"Daiquiri?" he asked with a grin revealing a gold tooth on one side.

"Yes, that's it!" I sighed in relief. "And the other wants an iced tea." I expected that was like the cold tea we drank at home, but had no idea what the strawberry thing was.

The bartender mixed liquids from different bottles and poured the results into a shallow glass with a long stem, and wider at the top than the bottom.

"The pitchers of tea and ice water are near the drink dispensers." He gestured to the back wall with the glass before handing it to me. "I'm Phil, by the way."

"Bet." When his eyes narrowed, I explained, "That's my name. Bet." I took the drink, then went and poured the tea from a pitcher into a regular glass, and brought both to the table by the window. Someone now sat at another of my tables. After placing the drinks in front of the two women, I approached the man at table three. He was young with curly blond hair framing a pleasant face.

"Are you new here?" he asked. His smile didn't reach his bright blue eyes. They seemed to examine every inch of me.

"This is my first day."

"Well, you have to be better than the one who was here yesterday." He rolled his eyes. "Prettier too." Pink spots appeared in his cheeks.

"What would you like to drink?" I had heard Carolyn ask one of her customers that.

"Beer." He went back to perusing the card like the one the two women had consulted, dismissing me for the moment. Returning to the bartender, I asked for a beer for my new customer.

"What kind?"

Phil's question took me by surprise so I shrugged. "He just said beer."

Looking at the young man and nodding, he took a glass from behind him and filled it by pulling down a handle. "Anything else?"

"Not right now." I carried the beer carefully, knowing too much movement would disturb the bubbles on the top. I delivered it and the customer ordered a burger with everything. Before I returned to the kitchen, I asked Carolyn about the computer and she showed me how to use it. I'd never seen such a thing before, but after the other wonders of this world, it was just one more for me to master.

There was so much for me to learn.

CHAPTER 9.

The rest of the day passed like a blur. I tried to remember what each person wanted, but resorted to writing everything on paper the way Carolyn and the other waitress did. The cooks gave me the right meal when I did, and it made it easier to use the computer, which spit out a small paper strip with the items listed and the price.

I was most amazed, though, by how many of these customers paid. They handed me a shiny card, with a design, a name and a number appearing on them. Some even included a blurry picture that looked enough like the person to confirm it belonged to them. Carolyn showed me what to do with the cards.

The few customers who paid with currency were easier. I'd always been good at math, so I was able to go to the drawer where the bills and coins were kept, and bring them the difference between what they gave me and the amount they owed. I was surprised the first time one of them left some money on the table. Carolyn said the currency belonged to me because they were pleased with my service.

"You mean I can keep it?" I was afraid to touch it.

She nodded. "It depends on how they handle tips here. The people who use credit cards leave tips, too, usually on the slip they sign. The owner or manager will give us our share when they pay us. Remember I asked him about how they handle tips?"

"Oh!" This was better than I expected. It seemed like so much money compared to the little I had but then I thought about how much the customers paid for their food.

A lull in the flow of customers soon led to an empty restaurant. I'd served over fifty people by the time the restaurant closed that night. When had it turned dark outside? I couldn't remember eating anything besides my apple all day, and my stomach noises demanded that it be fed.

Once the restaurant closed its doors, I followed Carolyn into the kitchen. Phil, the bartender, and Allie, the other waitress, had a plate of food in their hands. One of the cooks handed us each a plate of whatever was left over in the pots and pans. I took a forkful of a mixture of meat and beans in a reddish-brown sauce. At the first bite. my mouth suddenly caught fire and my eyes dripped. The cook gave me a glass of water, and I drank it down without stopping to breathe. It only helped a little. "What did I just eat?" I croaked out.

Everyone laughed at me. "That, my friend, is chili." Carolyn covered her mouth but it didn't hide her grin.

She and the others explained about the potent peppers used to prepare the dish. Then Allie told me to eat the bread on my plate. It didn't have the crunch or the nutty flavor of my mother's bread, but it did make my mouth feel like it was no longer on fire.

The manager, Hal Parker, joined us as we finished. He handed a white envelope to each of us. Inside mine I found more of the greenish paper used for money here. When I added up the amounts on each kind of currency, I realized I had a hundred and fifteen dollars to add to the 'tips' I'd received from customers.

"You two did well today. I'll see you back tomorrow." And with that, he left.

As Carolyn and I walked out, I asked, "Is this our pay?"

She smiled. "Honey, those are your tips for the day. Before we return to the restaurant tomorrow, I'll take you shopping for clothes."

She sounded like Aunt Gill. Why did everyone think they needed to tell me what to wear? I looked at Carolyn in her blue pants and shirt, this top with a picture of a rainbow on it, and then down at my long full skirt and buttoned shirt. Maybe she was right.

"Your skirt's too long, and the outfit you wore

yesterday? It could have come straight from the eighteenth century." She linked her arm in mine as she'd done earlier in the day. "Tomorrow, we'll get you some trendy clothes. Like mine."

It was nighttime as we walked back to the Y, but not as dark as it was at night on Nokar. Tall poles along the street held a glowing torchlight at the top, but they weren't lit by fire. The vehicles that passed also had lights at the front and rear that cast long shadows on the ground. I'd wondered how the lamps in the restaurant were lit. Did these work the same way?

Almost as many people filled the streets as at midday, still rushing in every direction. And just as many vehicles.

"We could take a bus back to the Y, but it's such a nice night, we should walk." Carolyn started off without waiting for me to answer.

A bus. That was what the larger conveyances were called. The ones that carried many people.

We arrived back at the Y and Shelley sat at her desk. "Carolyn says I have enough for one more night and a breakfast card for three days." I handed her the money. "Tomorrow I should have enough to pay for two more nights." I hoped it would be enough time to find Rolf, but I still had to find a way to make sure one of the remaining apples led me to him and the portal key rather than someone, or something, else that wasn't from this place.

I felt as tired as I'd ever been, especially my feet, and went up to my room. Monique was where I'd left her, sitting at the table, her fingers tapping on the letters on the machine on her desk and occasionally looking at the words that showed up on the upright board in front of her. I'd thought of some questions to ask that wouldn't show my ignorance. "What do you hope to accomplish with your work?"

She hadn't heard me enter, because she turned to me with a start. "Bet, you're back!"

"Yes. Carolyn and I worked at a restaurant most of the day so I now have enough to stay another night." I hoped she wasn't put out that I'd stay another day.

"Then it's good you left your belongings here. I'm writing the great American novel." She indicated the words. "Well maybe not American, since it takes place in England."

If I wasn't mistaken, that was one of the places Carolyn thought I came from.   "Oh, how wonderful!" I'd read a few novels in my life. It must take a strong imagination and persistence to produce one. "What is it about?"

"*Country Girl* is a historical romance, about a great love affair in the eighteenth century, but it's taking so much more research than I thought it would. I have to google all sorts of facts."

I wasn't certain I'd heard her correctly. What sort

of word was 'google'?

She smiled at me. "It's amazing what you can find on google."

So this 'google' was used to find things. Perhaps I could use it to find Rolf. Unfortunately, I wouldn't know where or how to start.

"I'll have to eliminate a lot of facts that clutter the story." She told me how she searched for what she needed to write her book. Information on clothing and customs, foods and lifestyle. "My heroine is a farm girl who travels to London to seek her fortune and finds love. But she's not prepared for the differences in the big city."

That sounded familiar. It sounded like my life but even more like the book Fiona, the dressmaker, had mentioned. But it couldn't be, because that would mean someone had been here from other worlds. Still, several ideas took shape in my mind as she spoke. For one, if I could 'google' to eliminate the other things that didn't belong in this world, that were...what was the word again? Oh, yes...alien but known to the people here, what was left would be Rolf and the key!

When Monique finished her explanation about her work, I dared to ask, "Can you show me how to 'google' something? It might help me find my countryman."

Her eyes narrowed shrewdly. "And what will I get out of this exchange?"

What did I have to give her? Carolyn had said that

the clothes I'd worn the day before were like the ones they'd worn in the eighteenth century, and I came from a farm. I smiled thinking about my other idea. "I might be able to help with your story. I expect I know about some of the things you're looking for."

She stared at me for a full minute before nodding. "You just might. Did you ever live on a farm?"

I nodded and smiled. "That's where I grew up."

"And everything here in New York is new to you?"

"Yes it is." It felt good to tell the truth in this world for once. "Then there's the dress I wore yesterday."

"Oh yes!" Her slanted eyes flashed with excitement. "You can be a big help to me, and in return I'll show you how to use a search engine. Not just google, but the others too." She had me sit at the table. "Okay, what do you need to know?"

I'd have to be careful about what I told her. I didn't think she'd believe me if I said I came from another world. She'd think I'd lost my senses, and then she wouldn't want to help me. I wished Aunt Gill or Morgan, who'd done this before, had instructed me on what to tell the people I met in the lands I visited. I wanted to know whether there was a list of objects and beings that didn't come from this world and where they were kept, so I could avoid them, but what I said was, "I need to know where you put alien...people."

"Illegals? Did your countryman come here without

a passport?"

How could I answer if I didn't know what a passport was, or even what she meant by 'illegals'? I took a chance. "Yes."

She shrugged. "I suppose they're held in jail until they can be deported. That is if they're caught."

"Oh." I frowned. This wasn't producing the information I needed.

"If you're looking for a specific person, and you know his name, you can search on that," Monique said. "Of course, that assumes he used his own name."

"OK." I was taking a chance, but I didn't think I had a choice. "His name is Rolf Peters."

"Then type his name into the computer and we'll see if we can find him. Just hit the keys with the letters."

This was a different kind of computer from the one at the restaurant. I looked at the board in front of me. The letters were a jumble, but I found the right ones and slowly spelled out his name.

"Now press 'enter'."

It took me a little time to find the button with the word 'enter' instead of one letter. But when I pressed it, I could read in front of me 'About 7,000,000 results'. I couldn't believe my eyes.

CHAPTER 10.

Monique peered over my shoulder at the results. "Guess Rolf Peters is a more common name than I thought." She tapped my shoulder to indicate I should let her sit again. I stood and she took my place. Somehow she made the words on the screen move. "These are mostly Facebook and LinkedIn pages for people with that name."

I squinted and read those words in tiny print, but had no idea what they meant.

"Aren't you on Facebook?" She raised an eyebrow as she turned briefly to stare at me.

I slowly shook my head. What a strange world.

"I bet if we googled your name we'd get lots of hits." She touched the letters to spell 'Bet'.

"It's actually Anabet. Anabet Haines." I could see my name appear on the part she called a screen as she tapped each letter.

"Haines with an 'I' or a 'Y'?"

"I."

But when she finished, all of the 'hits' were for

people named Haines but not Anabet: Annette, Annabel.

"Did you ever google your name?" I asked.

She tapped out Monique Cho. Over 2,000,000 hits. "Not as unique as you, I guess."

"Can we go back to finding Rolf?"

Monique pursed her lips. "There are so many illegals, who come to this country from all over, hoping for a better life."

"What? Oh!" I guess she meant people from other countries, not other worlds. "What do you call anything that's not from this world?" I dared to ask.

"You mean like men from Mars? ET? Extraterrestrials?"

I nodded. "Can we search for those?"

She studied me with a twisted smile. "You realize there really aren't any, Roswell, Area 51, and movies notwithstanding?"

"Huh?" I rubbed the sides of my throbbing forehead as I thought, searching for something I knew a little about. "I mean things like meteorites."

"Oh, you mean objects. Does your friend have something from out there?" She waved her arm and pointed upward.

He had something from another world, so it was true when I said, "He's not my friend, and yes."

"And that's why you're looking for him?" Her eyes were slits.

"Yes." At last, something I could agree to without feeling guilty.

Her eyes opened wide again. "Maybe something like a moon rock? Is it valuable?"

"It's valuable to the government of my land."

She nodded and her gaze returned to the screen. "Let's see what we can find about extraterrestrial objects."

But it appeared there was extensive debate over whether there was life anywhere besides this world. There also wasn't any complete inventory of objects that came to this world, what people here called Earth.

"Well, thank you for trying Monique." I sighed and flopped onto my bed.

"Does this mean you won't help me with my research?" Her shoulders stiffened.

"What? Oh, no, of course I will! We agreed you would show me how to look for Rolf and...and what he has, and you did. It's not your fault it didn't work. I promised I would help you. You've fulfilled your part, now it's my turn."

She relaxed. "Thanks."

"So, what did you want to know?"

"Okay, where to start? What's it like to work on a farm?" She looked back to the machine, hitting letters as I spoke.

I sat on the edge of my bed. "In the spring, we plant vegetables. We also have some animals to tend to.

When I left, our cow was ready to calve." I still felt sorry I would miss that. "And in the late summer and fall we harvest our crops." I hoped the same was true on an eighteenth century farm here.

"What did you like best and least on the farm?" she asked. "I need to include real emotions for my heroine."

I had to think about that. My view had changed since I left home. But I knew what I missed. "I loved working with my parents and brother. I guess you'd call it a feeling of belonging, of being family. The worst? I guess it was hard work, but I didn't mind that so much. Maybe the worst was never leaving the farm; I couldn't see the world, and I so much wanted to do that. Just as you said your heroine did."

She turned to look at me. "But you've left it now."

"Yes, yes I have, and nothing is like I expected."

She nodded. "The Big Apple isn't what I expected either."

"The what?" I scratched my head.

"Haven't you ever heard anyone refer to New York City with that phrase?"

"Oh, of course," I lied. I didn't like becoming more adept at fibbing, but it was all I could do. Did Cass' apple key bring me here because of the name? But that would mean that portals could lead to a different place, depending on the nature of the key, and Gill told me something different. Monique stared at me and I had to say something. "What did *you* expect when you came here?"

Monique shrugged and smoothed her already smooth black hair, a gesture I was coming to associate with her. "I thought I'd walk into the offices of a publishing house, hand them the manuscript I'd been working on all the way through college, and receive a contract on the spot. It doesn't work that way. The first three editors wouldn't even see me, and the fourth laughed in my face. I realized what I'd written wasn't so special after all. Or rather, there were tons of other young writers vying for their attention. And many had agents who could pave the way for them."

"Oh!"

"So how did the city strike you when you arrived?" She leaned back in her desk chair and twisted her neck back and forth, rubbing it.

"The first things I noticed were the crowds, the noise, the..." I groped for the word Carolyn used about the vehicles passing to and fro, "...the traffic! So many people in one place, so many tall buildings, but most of all, the energy of the place."

"Yes, everyone's always hurrying to go somewhere. Have you been in the subway yet?" She rolled her eyes.

"The subway?"

"Guess not. Well, there'll be time for that. Right now we need a strategy to find your friend." She rolled her chair closer to the table again and began tapping the letters.

"I told you. He isn't my friend."

"Did you? Well, it doesn't matter. Wait, you were sent to find him because he stole your country's extraterrestrial thing, right?"

"Yes. He's a thief, and my government gave me the mission to find him and the...thing."

"Is it bigger than a breadbox?"

"Pardon?" Really, she said the most extraordinary things.

Monique laughed. "It would help if I knew how big this 'thing' is."

No one ever told me what the original key looked like. I had always thought of it as a real key, but of course, like my apples, it could be in any form.

"It had to be small enough for Rolf to carry it easily. Probably small enough to hide."

"So we're not looking for some massive stone or anything. What DO you know about it?" she asked.

"Only that it's not from this world." I shook my head. "I'm sorry I asked for your help. This is my task and I'll fulfill it on my own."

"Oh, Bet, how do you think you can do that when you don't know your way around?" She reached out her hand, gently catching my arm.

"I...I..." I couldn't tell her about the apples and how

I was supposed to use them.

"Maybe we'd better sleep on it," Monique suggested. "Who knows what our dreams might tell us." She touched a letter and the screen went dark.

I thought about the dream I had before I left home. As I washed up and changed into my nightdress, I wondered whether that was a clue and, if so, whether I could rely on it. Would I find what I looked for in the dinner party, the seashell or the beach? I fell asleep, still reviewing what I remembered about the dream.

CHAPTER 11.

In the morning I still had no idea of how to proceed. I could always bite another apple and hope for the best, but I wanted assurance I'd be successful.

Across the room, Monique, already awake, worked at her computer. Her fingers flew over the buttons. Letters, words, entire paragraphs appeared above on the screen.

She turned to me. "You're awake."

I nodded, rose and walked towards the door. "Have you thought of anything to aid me in my quest?"

"I had an idea, but I'm not sure it'll help. When did Rolf arrive here? Do you know?" She turned back to her machine in preparation rather than dismissal.

"He arrived less than a week ago." I reasoned Aunt Gill hadn't known about the theft when she arrived at the farm for me, so it happened while she was on her way to or from the farm. "How can knowing that help?"

"We can try a new search, limited by time, on anyone who entered the country from...where did you say you were from?" She waited for my reply.

Uh-oh. How could I answer? Maybe by pointing out the futility in basing a search on where he said he was from when he arrived. I pressed my lips together before replying. "If he entered illegally would there be a record? And how will we know where he went once he was here?"

She frowned. "Good points."

I hoped she didn't hear my sigh of relief. "He'd have to find lodgings as I did. Perhaps we can ask at places he might be staying."

"Good idea. Maybe he went to the YMCA near here." She smiled. "We can check after breakfast."

"Is the YMCA the place where men stay in the Big Apple?" I liked that name for this city. It reminded me of my green portal key and the red ones that should have led me to Rolf. "I can go by myself and ask for him." I could use an apple to find out whether he was there if I was alone.

"Don't you want help? I can show you where it is, and ask the right questions." Her eyes shone with eagerness to assist me. How could I refuse? But that would create a new dilemma. If she was with me, could I use the apple? I'd have to try.

"Thank you." I smiled back. "Let's go."

"Okay, but first breakfast." She pushed a button and the words went away from the screen, then she stood and grabbed a short black skirt and long black top.

We took turns using what Monique called a shower and then dressed. I chose another of the dresses Gill bought me, even though it would stand out among the clothing these people wore. Then again, Monique's attire differed from that of everyone else as well.

We took the elevator down, and she led me to a large room, filled with long tables with benches on either side. "We get our food from over there." Monique pointed to a door with only the top half open. A woman stood on the other side, handing plates of food to everyone who passed. We showed our breakfast cards and each received a plate.

The food was similar to what I ate at home. After my experience at the restaurant the day before, serving and finally eating unfamiliar dishes, it was comforting to breathe in the aroma of sausage and eggs, toasted bread and porridge. On our way to a table, Monique stopped to pour coffee from a huge metal container.

"Do you drink coffee or tea?" she asked.

I had liked the coffee I drank at Clair's and at Morgan's, but I much preferred tea. "Tea please."

She handed me a heavy white cup of hot water and a paper packet with a little string attached. I turned it this way and that and my eyes narrowed. There were tea leaves in the packet and I was supposed to put it into the water. A clever way to make just one cup of tea!

We found seats together. I smiled seeing Carolyn

on the other side of the table. She sat with the two women I met the first night at the Y. I tried to recall their names, but all I remembered was that they had names like boys.

"After we eat, I'm taking Bet to the YMCA to see if she can find her countryman there," Monique announced.

"Maybe I'll go with you, and then Bet and I can continue on to the restaurant." The shirt Carolyn wore had a drawing of a boy with very yellow hair and the words 'Eat my shorts'. I wondered if he meant shortbread or something else.

"Bet, can I tell them what you said about the guy you're trying to find?" Monique asked.

I felt pleased she wouldn't say anything without asking my permission. "Yes, it'll be all right if you do."

"He stole some kind of extraterrestrial object and Bet's government wants it back." Monique's voice held increased excitement. "That's why she's here."

"Ooooh! You're a spy!" the woman with the dark skin said and her almost black eyes developed a gleam. Willy was her name.

I shook my head, although it was possible that part of Aunt Gill's missions had been to spy on the new worlds she visited. "I'm only a traveler and sometimes a courier." I pressed my lips together, still uncertain of how much to reveal. "This mission is very important to our ruling council." I hoped they had councils in this world.

"Then we'll all help you achieve it!" The blond's eyes flashed too. "Kind of an adventure."

I suddenly remembered her name, too. "Danni, it might be best if only Monique and I go, and perhaps Carolyn."

"Oh, that's just to scout out the situation. That's cool." Willy nodded. "But when you corner the thief and get back what he stole, it'll be better to have some back-up, don't you think?" Her voice sounded eager.

I looked at Carolyn and Monique for guidance. I had no idea what she meant. They both smiled, so I took a chance and nodded.

"C'mon and eat," Monique urged. "Your food is getting cold and we have some scouting to do."

I cut a piece of sausage and put it in my mouth. My tea was strong and still hot, but the bread with my meal was as tasteless as the eggs. "What kind of bread is this?" I waved a piece in the air.

"Oh, it's just packaged white bread. Not very good," Carolyn said. "People like the restaurant because they bake their own bread daily."

"Wow!" Danni said. "I'll have to try the place. Fresh bread is hard to come by."

"It's called Satellite, over on Broadway," Carolyn told her.

"Don't people make their own bread here?" Another surprise to add to all I'd had.

Monique smiled at me and told the others, "She grew up on a farm," as if that explained everything.

I learned little more during breakfast. Both Danni and Willy worked in an office and had to leave as soon as they finished eating. "We'll see you all this evening. Hope you find Bet's friend."

After breakfast, Monique and Carolyn led me to the Y for men not far away. As we approached, after a bit of hesitation and uncertainty, I took a red apple from my draw-string bag and took a bite.

"Hungry already?" Monique asked. "You just had breakfast."

I shrugged because I had found that when I did, her questions ceased. A light beam appeared, as it had the day, before but led in the opposite direction from the way we were going. How could I follow it? Would it lead me to another alien in this world instead of Rolf? I took a step toward it.

"Bet, stop dawdling!" Carolyn called to me. She and Monique stood quite a distance ahead of me on the street.

Two things I knew for certain. They didn't see the beam, and since it was leading away from the YMCA, Rolf wasn't there. I walked quickly to catch up to my new friends. "I don't think we'll find him here," I said.

"Why not?" Monique asked.

I shook my head. "Just a feeling."

We walked through the doors into a reception area

very similar to that at the women's Y, except the man sitting behind the desk looked nothing like Shelley. He was bearded and scowled. In a surly voice he asked, "What do you dames want here?"

Carolyn took the lead. "We're looking for a friend of Bet's." She nodded toward me. If I corrected her about being Rolf's friend, it might be harder to prompt the man to talk to us, so I remained silent.

"Name?"

"His name is Rolf Peters, but he might have used another name," I said.

"Name's not familiar. What's he look like?"

Why hadn't my aunt or someone else described him to me? I had only an impression of his appearance, but since I was convinced he wasn't there, it didn't matter. "Tall and blond. He would have arrived within the week."

The man shook his head, then grinned as he told us, "He's not here, and never was."

Carolyn and Monique frowned, more disappointed than I was.

"We'll have to think of some place else to look, but right now we'd better get over to the restaurant." Carolyn took my arm.

I nodded, but I began to worry I'd never be able to find Rolf, especially when we walked outside into the hot street. The light beam was gone. And I only had one red apple left.

CHAPTER 12.

That day at the restaurant was a little easier. I knew what to expect. A few customers I served the day before returned, and when I remembered what they'd ordered, they smiled. I loved feeling I was becoming a good waitress.

But not everyone I served were so pleasant. "I want an iced tea with a slice of lime. Not lemon!" an older man insisted. I collected his drink and brought him another with a lime slice in it.

"You call this a lime?" He held up the section of fruit and waved it in my face. "It's dry." He licked it and winced. "And sour."

"I'll bring you another one, sir." I returned to the drink dispenser and looked in the bowl of lemon and lime slices for a juicier piece, but they all looked the same. I noticed the day before the bartender also had fresh cut fruit behind the bar. Fortunately for me, that day he had fresher limes. I delivered a slice to my customer, but he never thanked me.

After the lunch crowd finished their meals, the restaurant emptied. The young man, who was one of my first customers the previous day, came in and took the same table, number three.

"Did you wish another burger and a beer?" I waited with my pad to take his order.

He stared at me, then back at the menu. "No, today I will try the chicken Parmesan hero." He pronounced it very carefully. It was the third item on the list, after the turkey sandwich and the burger.

I smiled. "Are you making your way through our menu?" At his blank look to my attempted humor, I let it drop. "What about another beer? The same kind as yesterday?"

"Is there more than one kind?" His eyes narrowed, but I showed him the back of the card where ten different brews were listed. "Oh!"

I waited patiently as he ran his finger down the list.

He shook his head. "Whatever you brought me yesterday...that will be fine."

"Very good, sir." I went to order his meal, but glanced back in time to see his gaze roam over the restaurant. What, or who was he looking for?

The sandwich I brought him oozed cheese and tomato sauce. It smelled of oregano and garlic. He examined it before opening his mouth very wide to take a bite. He chewed, then smiled. "This is very good."

Had he never had this kind of sandwich before? I hadn't, but I would have expected a native of this land to have eaten one. He wiped red sauce from his mouth once with his napkin, and then continued to eat. Before long, I was too busy to think about him anymore.

That evening, the restaurant was busier than the day before. By closing time, my legs and back ached and I longed to sit down. My stomach growled, too. I walked back to the kitchen to join Carolyn, who was already eating. I may have been exhausted, but when the manager came by with our pay and tips, I thought how it was all worth it.

"That'll be enough for you to stay at the Y for a few more days," Carolyn told me.

I nodded. I could make another attempt to find Rolf Peters, but I only had one red apple left, along with the green apple that would take me home, and no clear plan for how to use the red one.

Carolyn and I returned to the Y and I bid her goodnight before I went to my room. Monique sat at her machine. I yawned and waved but didn't have the energy to chat. All I wanted was my bed.

During the night, my mind wandered to what Leone said about Rolf crossing the portal to look for a weapon that the rebels could use. I knew nothing about weapons on Earth. I resolved to ask Monique and Carolyn about that in the morning.

When I woke, Monique sat at the table again, using her computer to write her story. She had a red apple in her hand and was about to take a second bite out of it with her dainty white teeth.

I squinted to see it clearly. "Is that...is that one of my apples?" My voice sounded high and loud even to me.

Monique dropped the fruit, clearly as startled as I was. She stared at me and picked up the apple. "I didn't think you'd mind." She shrugged. "It's just an apple and you've been carrying it around for a few days. You can get a fresh one downstairs." She took her bite and began chewing.

Tears welled up in my eyes, but what could I say? "I didn't mean to shout at you." I could barely breath, let alone speak. It wouldn't help for me to scream at her. She couldn't know how important that apple was to me. I was grateful it wasn't the green one. The beam of light failed to appear. I tried to breathe and speak normally. Having hysterics at this point wouldn't bring the rest of the apple back.

I don't think it was my voice, but rather the frown on my face that caused her to stop eating. "I'm sorry, Bet. I'd cut out the part I've been eating from and give the rest back to you, but I don't have a knife."

Would half an apple suffice for Cass' magic to work? It had only taken one bite to produce the beam, not the entire thing. I swallowed hard and looked through my pack for Morgan's knife. "I have one." Holding it up for her to see, I took the apple from her and cut it into two equal halves, returning the half she'd started with as much of a smile as I could manage. My half joined the green apple in the bag.

"Aren't you going to eat yours?" The way her eyes narrowed and she stared at me indicated her curiosity about why the apple was so important, but I couldn't tell her.

"I don't want to spoil my breakfast." I patted the bag to reassure myself.

Breakfast was a repeat of the day before, with Willy and Danni offering to help with my search for Rolf. I refused again, as politely as possible. Afterward, Carolyn insisted on taking me to purchase 'jeans', as she called the trousers so many people wore. She grinned when I agreed to change from my skirt into them. By the time we finished our shopping, it was time to go to the restaurant to work. So, it wasn't until the afternoon lull that I had the opportunity to give that last half of the red apple a try.

The apple was turning brown on the cut face. I walked out of the restaurant and a short way to the street corner before taking a bite. A beam of light appeared immediately, and I sighed with delighted relief. I followed but it took me back inside the restaurant! Once inside, it led to one of my tables, occupied for the third day in a row by the strange young man with the piercing blue eyes. I froze momentarily. Could he be Rolf Peter?

I mustered my courage and approached the table. He looked my way, but his eyes were transfixed by something in front of me, the beam of light. Could he really see it? If he was Rolf, it was likely.

His gaze shifted to my face and his eyes widened.

"You see it too, don't you?" I put my hand in the beam, but it didn't stop the light.

He nodded. "Where does it come from?"

I thought about his question and about him. I swallowed but it didn't make my throat any wetter. "Are you Rolf Peters?"

"Who?" His forehead furrowed and he looked deeply into my eyes.

His lack of reaction to the name confirmed he didn't know who that was. And yet, the apple led me to him, and he could see the light. Was he also from another world? How much could I tell him?

"Rolf's a thief. He stole something from my government and I am trying to find him." I kept my voice low. There was no reason for anyone else to hear what we were talking about.

"What made you think I was this...Rolf?"

"I...I had an apple, enchanted to allow me to find anything or anyone who wasn't native to this world."

"Enchanted?"

I ignored his confusion. "You're not from this place,

are you?"

He hesitated, then shook his head. "May I assume you aren't either?"

I sighed. "No. Where are you from? What are you doing in New York?"

"I was sent by my sister to seek knowledge about the thresholds." He puffed out his chest.

I nodded. "You mean the portals between worlds."

"Ah, yes. You do know about those. Quite so." He smiled and his body relaxed. He was almost handsome.

"And you thought you could find that knowledge here, in this restaurant?"

"No, no. I return here each day to find the item I lost. Tell me, how did you come here?" His eyes hadn't left mine.

"To this world or to the restaurant?"

"Both, actually." He smiled again, and his face was suddenly much friendlier.

I looked around the place. There were only a few customers and Carolyn was serving them. "Let's walk outside. We're, uh, not supposed to talk with customers other than to take their orders."

He nodded and stood, then left. I followed him out and down the street. We stopped around the next corner. "I'm called Quint, by the way." He held out a hand.

If he was in a similar situation to mine, perhaps we could help each other. I shook the proffered hand. "I'm

Bet, and I'm from a world called Nokar. My government has been sending people through the portals for some time, perhaps even to your world. I was sent here to find a man who stole a portal key."

"This Rolf person you mentioned before?"

"Yes. I was given three enchanted apples. One bite would produce the light you saw and lead me to anything that didn't belong here. But there are other people and many items here that are from other worlds, including you." I shook my head and sighed. "What item were you looking for at Satellite?"

He hesitated. "My key." He looked down on the ground. "I lost it."

My throat constricted. I didn't know what I'd do if I lost mine. "How did you lose your key? What did it look like?"

"It was a fork. I had it on the table the first time I ate at Satellite and I believe it was collected with the plates and utensils when I finished eating. I must get it back, or I won't be able to return home!"

I nodded. "It might still be in the kitchen."

"Perhaps you can use one of your apples to find it." His eyes pleaded with me. "I don't know much about how magic works." He shrugged. "We're...we're not supposed to use it, which is why the Mothers refused to allow Zara, my sister, to use the key. I'm from Lamady."

"But you came here through a portal?"

"Actually, we didn't know about the portals until recently. And then, no one was willing to go through. Well, the Mothers objected. But my sister asked me because she couldn't do it. And my brothers wouldn't. I...I wanted to show them I was braver than they, even though I'm the youngest."

His world sounded fascinating. "Who are the Mothers?"

"The rulers of Lamady are called the Mothers. Actually, one is my birth mother."

"And the portal brought you to Earth."

He nodded. "My mission was to find out where the portal from Lamady led, and to learn how the portals work. But I lost the key. I can't go home until I find it."

Frowning, I said, "I could use an apple if I had any left. I...I've used them all. It was my third that led me to you."

"Oh, no!"

I looked at him, thinking about how I might help him. I was so lost in thought that I didn't hear Quint at first when he finally spoke. "What did you say?" I blinked.

"I know it's an imposition, but could you possibly help me?" he asked. "You have access to the restaurant kitchen. Perhaps you can look for the fork."

"I could, if I could distinguish it from all of the others in the kitchen." I glanced back toward the restaurant.

He knitted his brow. "The only distinguishing feature is that it has three tines instead of four."

My eyes widened. "Well, why didn't you say so in the first place?"

"You have seen it then?" His frown disappeared, and his eyes lit up.

I hated to disappoint him. "No. But I believe I can find a reason to look for it, and perhaps someone else has noticed it."

"You must be very brave to do that."

I blushed at his compliment. "I don't think it takes bravery at all, but an increasing ability to lie."

"You would do that for me? A stranger?"

If I couldn't accomplish my own goal, I felt an overwhelming need to help him. He was probably close to my age, thrust into a world he didn't understand and he seemed so helpless. And I thought I'd been unprepared for my assignment! "I can't promise anything."

"Oh, I realize that. Still, if it works, I could get on with my mission, knowing I can return to my world when I've completed my task."

"It might be best to try now when the cooks aren't as busy. Come back to the restaurant with me and order something, anything, so I'll have an excuse to go into the kitchen." I started back down the street.

Quint blinked and pressed his lips together. "Are you sure?" He walked beside me.

"No, but I have to try."

CHAPTER 13.

Quint smiled. "You're being very kind."

I rushed ahead of him, back to the restaurant, keeping pace with others around me. Fewer diners than before sprinkled the restaurant, and none at my assigned tables. When Quint entered, he took his usual seat.

"May I help you?" I pretended to suddenly notice him and made sure everyone around heard me.

He perused the entire menu, both front and back, taking his time. "I'll have the chili."

I shook my head. "Are you sure? It's very spicy."

"It is? Then I will have the noodle soup."

"Very good, sir." I wrote it down before hurrying to the kitchen. "A bowl of the noodle soup," I told Oscar, the sous chef in the afternoon. As he asked one of the others to get it, I addressed everyone. "Did any of you happen to see a three-pronged fork today?"

"I recall Andre using it this morning when he was preparing the cakes." Oscar indicated the pastry chef.

Andre nodded, running a hand through his wavy black hair. "It worked magnificently! I gave it to Carl to wash and leave at my station for tomorrow." He glared at the clean-up man.

Carl looked up from his sink, then shrugged his burly shoulders. "I don't know where it came from. We've never had one like it before."

But Andre checked his station. "It is not here."

Carl's hands went to his hips. "I put it with your whisks."

Andre shook his head and frowned. "Perhaps someone else used it, but they all know by now that no one touches my things." His strangely accented voice was rising.

"Is this what you mean?" Leo, the busboy, held up a fork.

"Yes, that is the one!" Andre snatched it from his hand with a snarl on his lips.

"It was in with the two-pronged lobster forks."

Andre rolled his eyes. "How did it get there?"

No one knew or was willing to admit to taking it.

"But why are you looking for it, Bet?" Oscar finally asked.

I expected someone would want to know and had an answer ready. "I told you I'm looking for a countryman of mine who stole some artifacts that my government wants back. I believe that fork is part of what he stole."

"But it's so perfect for working my frosting!" Andre objected.

I held out my hand. "If it isn't what I'm looking for,

I'll return it to you. I promise."

Andre frowned, but nodded and gave me the fork.

I smiled at him. "Thank you so much!" I took it and walked toward the swinging doors, but Oscar called me back.

"Aren't you forgetting something?" He held the bowl of soup I'd asked for.

"Oh, of course!" I took the soup and the fork back to Quint.

His eyes and mouth gaped open when he saw the fork in my hand. "You found it!"

"It was unusual enough that several people noticed it."

He grinned. "I don't know how to repay your kindness."

"Just eat your soup." I pointed at the steaming bowl. "We must keep up pretenses until you leave. I wish you well in your quest for knowledge about the portals."

"It would seem you know more about them than the people of this world." He was right.

"Perhaps when I return to my world, you can come with me and learn from my aunt and others who have made many journeys."

He stopped his spoon halfway to his mouth. "But first you must find your friend, Rolf."

"He's not my friend," I replied automatically. "In fact, I have never met him."

"Then how will you recognize him when you do?"

I sighed. "I don't know."

"If there is any way I can help, I would be most happy to."

I studied him. "Perhaps there is a way. Return after the dinner rush and we can talk about how we can help each other."

Quint nodded. He still smiled about the fork I retrieved for him as he absentmindedly spooned soup into his mouth.

CHAPTER 14.

After Quint left, I returned to the kitchen.

Carolyn followed me in. "I understand you've found an item your thief stole from your government."

At least she'd stopped calling Rolf my friend. "Um, yes. It was a special fork of historic importance."

"But I thought the things he took were alien." She peered through her eyelashes at me.

"Some were. The fork was old, back from the time of the monarchy." It was becoming easier and easier to spin tales to explain my actions. I hoped I wasn't becoming an accomplished liar. "I wonder whether this means he's been here."

Caro studied my face again. Perhaps she didn't believe me after all. Somehow that made me feel better about myself. "I have a feeling your customer has a crush on you."

"What?"

The corners of her mouth turned up. "The young man who always sits at table three. He's cute."

She must have seen us talking. I would have to be more careful in the future. "He seems lonely. He's new in the city, too. I wanted to make him feel comfortable."

She tsked-tsked. "We're not supposed to talk to our customers."

"I know." I shrugged. "Mostly he asked about the menu."

A number of people entered the restaurant for the start of the evening rush and we both went back to work. All through the dinner service I hoped Carolyn wouldn't ask to see the fork, and wondered what I could say if she did. But the restaurant was busier than the previous nights and I didn't have time to dwell on it.

When a couple I served demanded I take their food back because it wasn't hot enough, an older woman wanted another spoon because she'd dropped hers, and a group of young men became boisterous, all at the same time, I escaped to the kitchen for a breather. However, two cooks were in the midst of an argument over which of them burnt a souffle. Then Allie slammed a tray on the counter and took off her apron before running out of the kitchen yelling, "I can't work here any more!" And the head chef had his own fit. It wasn't any relief at all. Was everyone having a bad evening?

I took two deep breaths and returned to my tables. "Here you are." I placed a fresh dish of hot food in front of the man and removed the old one. I handed a new spoon to the older woman. "I hope this is clean enough."

She smiled. "Thank you, my dear."

Then I approached the young men. "Please

remember, you're in a public place. You're disturbing the other diners."

"Yeah? Guess we'll take our business elsewhere, then." One of them rose, followed by the others, and they stomped out.

I shrugged and turned to my other customers to make sure no one wanted anything else.

The manager called to me. "You'll need to cover some of Allie's tables."

I nodded. "I can serve some of them, even though mine are full." A couple had replaced the young men.

"Take fifteen, sixteen and seventeen. Carolyn can manage a few and I'll ask one of the kitchen staff to help with the rest." He shook his head. "This was not a good time for her to be so temperamental."

Allie was usually easygoing, taking everything in stride. It must have been more than a whim for her to leave so abruptly. I looked at the three additional tables I'd been assigned. The people at two of them were looking around. The woman at table sixteen was eating already and probably unaware that her waitress had departed.

I approached the couple at table fifteen and asked, "Have you decided what you want?"

"What happened to our waitress?" the woman asked. Her companion watched me intently, waiting for an answer.

"She had to leave unexpectedly. I'll be happy to

serve you. Please tell me what you want." I opened my order pad and smiled at them.

They both ordered burgers, medium rare, with a side of cole slaw. I was beginning to know what each of the dishes were and to devise my own abbreviations. "Very good. I'll have those out as soon as they're done."

The long-nosed man at table seventeen pushed his straw-colored hair from his eyes and stared at me.

"May I bring you something to drink?"

He looked me up and down. "You aren't from around here, are you? I thought not last night." He didn't sound like the natives either. In fact, he sounded more like the people at home.

"Are you from England, too?" It was a good guess because that was where everyone thought I was from.

"England?" He stroked his pointed chin. "Ah, yes, well." But he didn't say anything else.

"What would you like to drink?" I asked again.

"Water will do." He lifted the ice water in front of him and took a sip.

"Very good, sir." I turned but he called me back.

"Is that where you're from? England?"

I pressed my lips together, but at the same time I wondered why he'd asked. The way he worded it... "I'm sorry, we're not allowed to talk to our customers."

"No, of course not." He let me go but I felt his eyes on me. I fetched the pitcher of iced water and returned to refill his glass. "Do you know what you want to eat this evening?"

"Oh." His eyes returned to the menu. "Is the stew any good? Do they use fresh carrots and potatoes?"

"Yes, it's very good and full of vegetables."

"Then I'll have that. It's hard to find anyone who uses lots of fresh produce in this city."

I smiled. He was right, but our kitchen used only the best ingredients. "I'll have that out for you shortly."

It was quieter in the kitchen, everyone busy at their stations. The two men who'd argued earlier were each attempting to prepare the perfect souffle under the watchful eyes of the chef. "I need a bowl of stew," I announced.

Oscar ladled it out for me himself. I backed out of the kitchen, turned and started for table seventeen. The man was staring at me, studying my face. I placed the bowl in front of him. "Will there be anything else?"

He blinked. "You look like someone I know. The clothes you're wearing today are all wrong though."

He likely meant the jeans I'd bought that morning. I looked down at them. "Excuse me? What's wrong with what I'm wearing?"

"What is your name, my dear?" he asked.

My neck tensed at the familiarity and the oily tone of his voice. I considered refusing to answer and walking away, but he was a customer. "I'm called Bet. May I bring you anything else?" I looked around. "I do have other tables to cover, especially since your original waitress had to leave."

"No, nothing else right now. But come back in about fifteen minutes." He shifted his eyes from me to his food.

"Of course." I breathed a sigh of relief as I escaped. Checking my own tables, I saw that everyone was eating. The woman at sixteen had finished, though, so I asked her if she wanted dessert.

"Do I look like the sort of person who eats dessert?" she asked. "No, I want my check."

"Very good. I'll bring it right away." As I walked away, though, I realized I didn't have Allie's order book, and wasn't completely certain what the woman had ordered. She'd been eating the grilled chicken when I first saw her, but had she had an appetizer? What was she drinking? I looked for the manager to ask what I should do about the checks for Allie's customers, but he was nowhere in sight. Carolyn eventually helped me check the computer for the woman's order.

I finally returned to the man at table seventeen. He was almost finished with his stew, making good use of his cloth napkin to keep his face clean. "I hope you're enjoying your meal."

"I have had better, although you were correct about the vegetables." He studied me again, as he had earlier. I felt even more uncomfortable. "Remarkable how much you resemble Gill."

I fought to hide my surprise. He couldn't mean my aunt, could he? But I didn't look like her. Our coloring was the same, I suppose. "I don't know anyone by that name."

"Hmmm." He rubbed his chin and continued to study me.

"If there's nothing else I can bring you now, I'll be back shortly to check on you." I backed away. The less I had to do with this man, the better.

As I continued to serve my other tables, I thought through what he'd said. If he really meant that I looked like my aunt, then he had to know her. The only one in this city who could know Gillian was Rolf Peters! I glanced his way. Could it be? After worrying about how I'd find him, had he found me? Did he know I was here looking for him? Or was I just a waitress in a restaurant he frequented?

With three extra tables to serve, I was busier than ever. The man at seventeen lingered, then ordered desert, and then an after dinner drink. Each time I noticed him, my pulse raced. I thought he'd never leave.

By nine, I was able to take a breath. Customers remained at two tables, including the man at seventeen, but I could study him unobserved. Nothing about his appearance indicated that he was from anywhere but Earth. His accent was similar to mine, but he seemed more familiar with the food than Quint or I. That argued against him being Rolf.

At last, he left and so did the couple at one of my booths. The busboy cleared the last tables and I followed him into the kitchen, removing my apron.

"I hope Mr. Parker convinces Allie to come back," Caro said when she saw me. Her hair was coming out of it's clip and her eyes were half-closed. Her shoulders slumped. She leaned against a counter.

I collapsed on a metal chair along one wall and closed my eyes. My back and legs ached like never before.

"A little food should help." Oscar handed me a bowl of the stew I'd given the man at seventeen.

"Thank you." I took a spoonful, and chewed bits of tender meat and sweet carrot. Between trying to serve too many tables, and worrying about the strange man, I'd devised a plan to leave Carolyn so I could talk to Quint. After we'd both eaten some food I told her, "You were right about the young man." I wished I could blush on command to add authenticity to my feigned embarrassment. "He...he asked to meet me after we close tonight."

"Are you sure you'll be all right with him?" Her concern for me was sweet.

"Yes. He's very nice." I put a reassuring hand on her shoulder. "I'm safe with him, and he'll see me back to the Y."

She frowned."Okay. If that's what you want to do."

"If I haven't arrived by eleven, you can send out a scout to look for me," I joked.

"It's not funny!" She shook her head. "You don't know what some guys are like. A girl has to be very careful."

"I know, but Quint is OK."

"How do you know?" Her eyes narrowed. "How much do you know about him?"

I couldn't tell her, of course. I pressed my lips together, trying to think.

"Maybe I should go with you."

I sighed. "You can watch from the restaurant window. I don't think we'll go far." And that way, she couldn't hear what we talked about. I waited for her to agree.

"Well, all right, but if you do walk away together, I'll follow."

I nodded. We finished our stew and received our tips for the night. I took my money and my bag with the green apple out to the street, looking one way and then the other. I didn't see Quint. In fact the only one I saw was the man from table seventeen who might or might not be Rolf Peters. He leaned against a light pole, facing the door of the restaurant.

CHAPTER 15.

I stared at the man from the restaurant. My shoulders tightened and I tried to think clearly. I took a few unsteady steps away from him. If he was Rolf, and he probably was, I wasn't prepared to deal with him out here on the street, yet I needed to confirm whether he was the man I'd been looking for. I stopped and looked back.

"Ah, Miss...what did you say your name was?" The man came closer.

"B...B...Bet."

"Yes." His eyes narrowed. "Anabet, isn't it?"

I gasped. How did he know?

"Ah, yes, Gillian's little niece from the country. Tell me, child, who sent you after me?" His voice was low but I heard every word, even with the crowds passing by on the street.

"I...I don't know what you're talking about." I tried to stand tall, look him in the eye. The practice I'd had lately in lying should come in handy. But my eyes blinked faster than usual, and I couldn't stop them. Now I knew what they meant about a shiver up the spine.

"Was it the council? Sending a girl to bring me

back! What were they thinking!" His sneer changed to a nasty grin. "I'm not going back until I've found poisons with no antidotes anywhere on Nokar."

"Why are you telling me?" I hoped the tremor in my lips couldn't be heard in my voice.

"Why? Because you're going to help me procure them." He sneered again.

"Never!" I turned to go back to the safety of the restaurant, but he grabbed my arm and wouldn't release it. "Let go of me!" No one walking by responded to my shout. Tears burned my cheeks as I fought against him. He pulled me closer and I beat at his chest with a clenched fist. "Let me go!"

"I'm sure we can come to an agreement." He twisted my right arm behind me and seized the other, forcing me to walk away from Satellite.

I tripped over my own feet and would have fallen but he held me up. "We're not going far, just to a shop I know. Tell me, how could you follow me to this world when I had the only key? With another? What is it, and where?"

I refused to answer, biting my lip instead. My key was all I had and I wasn't about to share it. But why would he want to know what and where it was? If he had the original key, he didn't need mine. Or maybe... "Did you lose your key?"

He hesitated. "No, of course not. I have it in a safe

place."

I wasn't convinced. Besides learning to lie myself, I'd come to recognize the tell-tale signs. His eyes no longer met mine and his voice wasn't as controlled as at first. But if he no longer had his key, even if I could capture him, a big if, I still wouldn't have the original portal key.

We'd reached the corner where I talked to Quint earlier. Quint. What had happened to him? Then Quint shouted my name. I looked around.

"Sorry I was late." Quint ran towards us.

"Tell your friend to go," Rolf whispered in my ear. "Or he'll have to help us."

I didn't want Quint to be hurt so that was fine with me.

"Hi, I'm Bet's friend, Quint." He held out his hand, his face wearing a friendly smile.

"Quint, there's, uh, been a change of plans." My eyes shifted from one man to the other. "I need to speak to Rolf alone."

"But you said he wasn't..." He stopped as his eyes went wide.

"You told this man about me?" Rolf snarled.

Quint blinked, then swallowed. "As I said, I'm Bet's friend. If you hurt her in any way, you...you'll have to answer to me." His bravado didn't fool anyone, especially since his voice rose to a higher pitch.

"Quint, you'd better leave." My eyes pleaded with

him to do what I said.

He pursed his quivering lips. "Are you sure?" His eyes never left Rolf's face.

"Quite sure. I'll see you tomorrow."

"All right, if you insist." With hands stuffed in his pockets he walked back toward the restaurant and I sighed with relief.

"You did that well." Rolf tugged on the arm he held tightly. "Now, I hope, you'll do the rest as well. Let's go before any other knights come to your rescue."

I had no choice but to go with him. At least Quint was safe, unless he decided to do something foolish.

"It's not far to an all-night store where we can purchase everything I want, and then you'll get me back to Nokar so I can give the poisons to Orson Henry."

"So you did lose the key!" I clutched the strings of my bag.

"Not lost." He sighed. "Misplaced. I suppose it won't hurt to tell you, since I already admitted I need your key." But he didn't say more.

We crossed to the next street. The lights shone in one of the shops, a pharmacy. Rolf pulled me towards the door and then inside. "Tell them that you need drain cleaner."

"Is that a poison?"

"Oh, yes. And so is artificial nail remover. So many substances here that can harm people when used incorrectly."

"Artificial nails?" Had I heard him rightly?

"Not the nails but the liquid used to remove them." He extracted a paper from a pocket.

"Why don't you ask for them yourself?" Why did he need me? Surely he could purchase anything he wanted.

"Most of the items I want are usually bought by women." Rolf took a rectangular basket from a stack just inside the store with the hand holding the paper and continued to grip my arm. "It would appear strange for me to buy all of them."

I looked at the signs for each aisle of the store. "We can find the drain cleaner down that way." I pointed. The sooner I helped him, the sooner I could get away and find others to help me subdue him.

We walked along looking at the shelves, then stopped. "This will do. Toilet bowl cleaner." He had me pick up six containers and drop them in his basket, before we continued on.

"What will prevent me from telling the council about your plans when we return to Willoughby?"

He sneered at me. "Oh, *we* won't be going back to Willoughby. You're staying here with your new friend. Once I have enough poisons, you'll give me your key, and I'll return."

"I won't let you!" I stopped in my tracks, wrenched my arm free, and faced him. Shoppers rushed by, picking up merchandise and ignoring us. I folded my arms across my chest, glaring at him. "I...I'll destroy the portal before I would let you return." I didn't know how to destroy it of course.

"Oh, don't be such a child! There's more than one portal here. You can't destroy them all, especially if you don't know where they are." He was gloating.

My mouth opened wide. That wasn't what I'd been told. How did he know there was more than one? Had he found them? I shook my head but had no words. Quint's portal would take him to Quint's world, not Nokar.

"Let's finish here." He grabbed my arm again and spun me around to continue on. "You still need to tell me about your key."

That ignited the spark still inside me. "No! I won't." He could force me to help him purchase poisons from this store, but nothing would coerce me to divulge what he most needed to know.

"Of course you will. Once I'm through with you, you'll beg me to leave you and go back to Nokar, and you'll provide the means to do so." His eyes narrowed over a sinister grin. "I won't hurt you unless I have to, but you have no idea what I'm capable of."

We filled the basket with a few more poisons, then returned to the front of the store. Rolf paid for everything, never letting go of my arm. But as we left the store, a strange sight confronted us.

Carolyn and Quint waited outside, along with Oscar the sous-chef, Andre one of the cooks, and the bartender, Phil. They each brandished a long kitchen knife or rolling pin.

"Let her go!" Phil demanded. He appeared to lead the group.

Rolf laughed at him as he pulled out a knife of his own and held it against my throat. It pricked my flesh. "You can have her if she gives me her key!"

I gripped the bag with my apple even tighter. It didn't escape Rolf's notice.

"What's that? What do you have in the bag? Is it your key?" He removed the knife from my neck and used it to quickly cut the strings, snatching the bag before it fell. I darted away from him, but I couldn't let him have the bag. I reached for it and he slashed at my hand with the knife, drawing blood. Then he turned and fled with a bag of poisons and my only means to get home.

CHAPTER 16.

"Are you all right?" Quint asked, as I neared my friends.

Simultaneously, Caro and Oscar demanded, "What did he mean by a key?"

Andre crossed his arms and glared at me. "What was in that bag?"

I wanted to put my hands over my ears. Their concern was comforting, but I felt bombarded by their questions.

Phil put an arm around my shoulders and steered me towards the restaurant. "Let her catch her breath and she'll answer all of us."

I nodded and smiled gratefully at him. The time for lying to my friends here was over. If I had any chance of defeating Rolf and returning to my world, I'd need their help.

We entered the dark restaurant and walked through to the kitchen. Oscar turned on the lights. I smelled the pungent stew that had been cooking all day. We sat where we could.

"Most of you know I've been looking for Rolf. I...I haven't been completely honest about why. I owe you that truth." I looked at the face of my first friend in New York, Carolyn. "Yes, Rolf is a thief, but what he stole was an object that allowed him to pass from our world to yours."

Carolyn gasped. "World? How do you mean pass?"

Andre blinked. "What was the object? And what do you mean by your world?"

"Quint knows the whole story because he's also from another world." My gaze shifted to his face and I bit my tongue, but he didn't frown so he couldn't be angry I gave away his secret. "Best to start with the basics." Everyone stared at me with open mouths, wide-eyed stares or furrowed brows. "Where I come from, people have known about and used portals between worlds for about a hundred years, although I don't think any of them ever came here."

Andre shook his head. "You're punking us, aren't you, kid?" His usual accent had disappeared.

"I don't know what that means. But it's the truth," I insisted.

Phil clapped and chuckled. "Oh, very good. You're would-be actors, like half the young people who come to this town. Heck, I was one myself at one time. It didn't take too many lost roles to tell me I'd be better off as a bartender." He laughed louder. "Is this some kind of live role playing game?"

Quint grabbed my arm. "They don't believe us."

"At this point, it doesn't matter as long as they help." Then I caught the hurt look in Caro's eyes and took her hands. "I wanted to tell you, but I didn't think you'd believe me." I pointed to my neck. "These cuts are real Everything we told you is real."

Andre slapped the counter nearest him. "So you're not from England? I knew it!" He lowered his voice. "I knew it."

I chuckled at his insistence he hadn't been fooled even though less than five minutes before he hadn't believed me. It must have been hard for him to understand what I was saying so he probably latched onto something he could comprehend.

"A portal to this world was discovered recently, but before my government could officially send someone through, Rolf stole the key. Keys are needed to pass through the portals. They're usually not like ordinary keys, just as the portals aren't doors. Unfortunately, I still know little about the key Rolf stole."

"It wasn't that fork you were looking for earlier?" Andre's eyes narrowed. So much for him thinking he knew what was going on.

"That was mine." Quint held the fork up for all to see. "It's the key I used to get here. Bet was good enough to retrieve it for me." He smiled at me.

Carolyn wet a cloth napkin and came over to wipe off the dried blood from my neck and hand. Maybe it gave her a feeling that she was in control of the situation. "Now you have no way to return to your home." She stared into my eyes.

"Worse than that. Rolf has the poisons he wanted, along with my key so he can return to Nokar, and his rebel faction will have an advantage over the ruling government."

"Poisons? Was that what he wanted from the drugstore?" Phil shook his head. "But surely your people will have antidotes."

I shook my head. "Not for these. Rolf said he picked them because antidotes are unknown in our world."

"What did he buy?" Oscar asked.

"Mostly cleansers for drains and toilets. Something called artificial nail remover." I couldn't remember what else.

"Well, that's easy. If someone ingests any of those, they need to drink water or milk to dilute the poison and then vomit." Phil crossed his arms. Whether he believed me or not, at least he offered useful information.

"But there's no way for me to return and let the council know." I clenched my fists, trying to ignore the pain where my hand had been cut. "I have to stop Rolf before he passes through the portal." I looked at each of them. "Please help me."

"You know where it is." Quint started for the door. "Let's go there at once."

I shook my head. "He said there's more than one portal. I only know the one where I arrived."

"Was that just before we met?" Carolyn applied a strip across my cuts. It had a soft pad that she placed over the wound. The ends stuck to my skin. "On Park Avenue?"

"Yes."

Quint tilted his head and rubbed his chin. "Wait, what about his key? I thought he had the original."

I smiled, because it was just a little funny. "He misplaced it."

He nodded. "Which is why he needed yours."

Oscar's eyes lit up. "But if you can find his, you can go back to your planet!"

I didn't know what a planet was, but he had a point. How could I find the original key when I didn't know what it was, when he couldn't find it himself, and when I didn't have any apples left to lead me to it? "It's impossible!"

"Maybe not." Quint held up the fork again. "You helped me find my key."

"But I had an idea where that was, and I knew what it looked like." I frowned as I thought about how much more difficult it would be to find Rolf's key.

"What do we know about him?" Oscar asked.

"Only that he likes stew with crunchy vegetables." My frown deepened.

"Maybe we know more than that." Caro sat down on the chair I'd used earlier. Her eyes had a faraway look and then they focused again. "He's a man of habit, since he's eaten at Satellite every night that we've worked here."

"He has?" I didn't really notice him when he was Allie's customer.

"Did he pay by credit card tonight?" she asked.

I shook my head. "He used cash. Didn't leave a tip, either."

"Figures." Phil stroked his chin. "He always took the same table, near my bar."

"Did you notice anything unusual that could give us a clue?" Oscar asked.

The tension in my shoulders eased knowing at least some of these people accepted what I'd said, and even if they didn't, they wanted to help me. They'd risked their lives and now they were trying to find an answer to my predicament.

Phil had closed his eyes, but then opened them. "A hat. He had a hat with him the first night, but not tonight."

"Could that be his key, Bet?" Quint asked. "Maybe he came back like I did because he left it here."

"I don't know, but if it is, how will we ever find it?"

"Is there a lost and found here?" The excitement in

137

Carolyn's voice increased. "I'm sure people leave umbrellas and other items all the time."

"Like my fork." Quint caught her excitement.

"Only that was mixed in with the restaurant cutlery." Andre shook his head. "But a hat wouldn't be."

"I'll get the box of left-behinds." Phil went through the swinging kitchen doors.

I hugged myself and shivered. I'd been cold ever since Rolf grabbed me. "Somehow I thought Rolf's key might be a seashell."

"Why?" Carolyn handed me a chef's coat.

"Thanks." I smiled at her and put it on, but didn't reply. She was a good friend, and yet there were still some things I couldn't tell her.

Phil returned with a large cardboard box, and he and Oscar rummaged through it. They tossed out sunglasses, three mismatched gloves, and a black umbrella with a broken frame.

Oscar held up a man's brown knit hat. "Is this his?"

Phil shook his head. "It was a tweed fedora."

Oscar nodded and continued to search. "Bingo!" The hat was crushed but it still looked new. He handed it to me.

I twisted it around in my hands, but there was no way I could tell whether this was the portal key I sought. "I guess I'll have to see if this works."

"Now?" Quint took my hands to make me look at

him. "Bet are you sure you shouldn't wait until morning?"

"Now might be best. If it's night here it will be about the same time in Willoughby and the area around the portal won't be crowded so it will be easier to arrive unobserved."

"I'm coming with you!"

"Quint, you can't! We don't know whether the hat will work, and if it does, whether it can take two of us back."

"But you said your people have been using the portals for years. I can learn so much from them." His eyes shone, making his pleasant features handsome.

"And become caught up in the battle between the ruling council and the rebel faction." I shook my head. "You're not prepared for that."

"Who says? I'm as prepared for that as you were for this place!" Quint stood and glared, leaning toward me.

Carolyn pleaded softly with me. "Bet, maybe you should take him with you. Then the two of you could carry the antidotes you need."

"But where would we get them at this hour?"

Oscar laughed. "Remember, Phil told you all you'd have to do is have the victims drink lots of milk or water, and then force them to regurgitate. You do have milk and water where you come from, don't you?"

I nodded. "So I don't have to bring anything back." I looked at Quint. "And I won't need Quint's help."

The young man's face fell and he sat back down with a thud.

"Another time?" I offered, but that didn't cheer him.

Caro shook her head. "Oh, Bet, if you take him you'll find out whether the hat can work for two as well as one."

"Yeah, have pity on the kid!" Andre urged.

"You do remember he's the one who has the fork you were so keen on." I stared at him.

Andre shrugged. "I can find another."

I looked around at all the faces studying me and sighed. "Oh, all right. Come on Quint. We'd best be going." I sighed again, then hugged Carolyn. I doubted I would ever see her again.

Quint smiled but the expression didn't reach his eyes. "I...I'd like to get the rest of my things."

"So would I, but we don't have time. The sooner I return to Willoughby and report to the council, the better."

Carolyn joined us near the kitchen doors. "I'll walk with you."

"I will too, just in case," Phil insisted.

I turned to Andre and Oscar. "I'm sorry to leave when you're already one waitress short."

Oscar shrugged. "Mr. Parker will find someone else. Don't worry. Have a safe journey...or whatever you say to someone going through one of those portals."

Impulsively, I hugged Oscar and then Andre.

It wasn't a long walk across the park and then to Park Avenue. I found the spot where I'd arrived and led Quint to it.

He shook his head. "This isn't where I came to this world."

"That's another one of the portals Rolf mentioned. But it goes to your world." I felt a tear escape my eyes as I looked at Carolyn and Phil. "I can't promise to return."

"What should we do with your things?" she asked.

"Tell Monique to use my dress as a model for her book." I pressed my lips together. "You and she can divide the rest, or give the clothes to someone who needs them."

I stood on the island in the middle of the avenue with Quint at my side. I took his right hand with my left. "Ready?" When he nodded, I put the hat on my head. At first nothing happened, but then everything disappeared. Carolyn and Phil watching us, the cars and buses speeding by, and the tall buildings, all gone. The noxious smells and loud noises I had never become used to and the blazing lights that made it seem like daytime even this early in the morning.

Then there was nothing, no sounds, no odors, just my hand holding Quint's. At the last minute I yelled, "Duck!" and pulled him into a crouch.

CHAPTER 17.

"Ouch!" Quint rubbed his head where he'd hit it on the underside of General Mundsen's horse.

"I told you to duck." I covered my mouth to try to keep the laughter in.

"I thought you meant..." He stopped and looked around him. "So this is Willoughby."

"Only the waterfront." I watched his face for his first impressions. "Let's not dawdle here at the harbor. We have to find Cass, my aunt and the council and tell them what we know about Rolf." I rushed toward Cass' home with Quint following.

After a few streets, Quint stopped, holding his chest as he caught his breath. He held up a hand. "Slow down." He was taller than I, with longer legs, but I set a fast pace.

"We don't have time to see the sights. Later we'll show you around." The sun peeked over the horizon, bathing the quiet and deserted streets in pale light.

While we continued into the town, Quint chattered about what he saw. "This city is large, very different from my home. The buildings here are brick. And so are some of the roads. I say, that's an odd looking house, almost a hut isn't it?"

"That's where we're going. C'mon!" I marched up to the door and knocked, then listened for Cass' distinctive uneven footsteps.

"Who's there?" He'd become more cautious.

"Cass, open up. It's Bet." I bit my lip as I waited.

"Back already?" he asked through the door.

"It's been four days. And I have news."

The lock clicked. Cass swung the door wide and looked me over carefully before inviting me in. Then he glanced past my shoulder. "And who is this?"

"This is Quint. He's from another world. Not the one the portal led to, but still a different one. He's trying to learn as much as he can about the portals."

"Quite. Well, you'd both best come inside." He looked out but when he didn't see anyone else, he closed the door.

The place hadn't changed while I'd been gone. As cluttered as ever. "This is the key Rolf stole." I handed the hat to Cass, then sat in the same dainty chair I'd used before. Quint lifted some books from another chair, then sat with the books on his lap.

Cass examined the hat, rolling it around in his hands, but didn't say anything.

"I'm sorry but he got away from me with my green apple. He also has poisons that are unknown here and can be used as weapons without any antidotes here. They're used as cleansers in the world the portal led to."

"Oh, dear!" He frowned and shook his head.

"What happened here while I was gone? Why were you so reluctant to open your door?"

"The council and its soldiers chased Orson and his minions into the countryside and consolidated their position, but we all fear it's not the end of unrest." Cass paused. "And they still have Morgan."

I gripped the sides of the chair. "And by now they have the poisons. Does the council know where they've taken him?"

Cass shook his head. "But tell me more about the poisons." He put the hat on top of a tall pile of books and balanced on one of the other chairs. It threatened to fall off.

"On Earth, where I went, they are common enough, but they're nothing like what we use. If Rolf finds Orson and gives them to him, he might poison the councilors and try again to gain power."

"You must report to the council." He took another good look at me. One of his bushy eyebrows rose. "What *are* you wearing?"

I chuckled. "This is what the women wear on Earth." I stood and did a little pirouette. "There's lots to tell about the place, but now is not the time."

"I'll come with you to the council, and then take you back to your aunt's place. She's returned there, but she's been worried about you."

"As worried as she is about Morgan?" Before my journey through the portal and the events of the last few days, I wouldn't have dared talk to Cass that way.

He smirked. "Oh, both in equal measure. Well, times a-wasting. You'd best come, too. Quint is it?" He walked back to his door and we followed. "After you." He held the door open for us, and we hurried toward the building housing the council. When we reached it, Cass entered the chamber without knocking. Quint and I were close behind.

The council members sat at their table, all with clenched jaws or scowls on their faces as they talked in tight voices. Councilman Angus looked up when Cass led us through the door. "What is this..." Angus looked over his glasses. "Cass, do you bring us news?"

"Bet does." He ushered me forward. "Go ahead, young lady. Tell them what's happened."

"I believe Rolf returned to Willoughby with substances that are harmful if swallowed. I couldn't stop him. But I can tell you what to do if he or Orson use them."

Each of the council members stared at me. I

suddenly felt very small and abashed.

"And who is this with you?" Councilwoman Leone looked over my shoulder.

I nodded toward Quint. "This is Quint. He's from..." I looked at him quizzically. I didn't know the name of his world.

"I'm from Lamady. Bet was very kind to me on the world they call Earth. And I asked her to bring me here so I could learn more about the portals."

"Quint helped me when I fought with Rolf." I smiled encouragingly at my friend. "He was sent by his government to learn all he can about the portals."

Leone nodded. "Lamady did you say? I believe one of our travelers visited his world."

Angus tapped his chin. "Oh, yes. I remember now. That's one of the places Clare went some time back. But no one had been to Earth before."

"I believe Rolf and I were the first, and that the people there know nothing about the portals. Well, now a few do, the ones who helped me return here. But I didn't think it was my place to spread the word about the portals in such a populated place."

"We want to hear what you can tell us about Earth." Leone folded her hands. "You'll need to make a full report."

I nodded. "I intend to. But first, I must tell you how to treat anyone who is poisoned by the substances Rolf brought back. The victims must drink water or milk as soon as possible to dilute the poison, then regurgitate whatever they've swallowed."

Councilman Liam leaned forward. "Are the poisons that lethal?"

"Oh, yes. I can't emphasize it enough."

Leone dismissed me. "Well, thank you Bet. You've performed your assignment quite well for your first time traveling, despite your incomplete training."

I didn't think I had. "Do you want me to tell you more about Earth right now?"

"It can wait." Leone turned to the others on the council. "We have more pressing issues."

I narrowed my eyes, trying to fathom what was happening. "I'm glad I could return and warn you, and I'm prepared to make my full report whenever you're ready."

Angus held up a hand. "Later you can make your report. Cass, please take Bet to her aunt's apartment."

"What about Quint?" I glanced at him, reluctant to leave if he stayed.

Angus stroked his beard before replying. "We have some questions for your young friend."

Quint put a hand on my shoulder. "It's all right, Bet. I have questions for them, too. Perhaps I'll see you later. And thanks once more for finding my key."

I licked my lips, I had my own questions for the council, but not now. "Thank you, too. I will see you again.

That I am sure."

"Come, Bet." Cass took my arm and led me out of the chamber.

I studied the ground as we walked toward Aunt Gill's apartment. "I hope he'll be OK."

That eyebrow shot up again. "What kind of word is that?"

I looked at him. "You mean 'OK'? The friends I made on Earth used it to mean 'all right'." I smiled slightly. "I like it."

"Did you like that world?"

"Some things about it, yes. Very much. Such wonderful technology! And some of the people were very kind indeed. But there were so many of them! And the noises and the smells!"

"You'll have to tell us everything."

I nodded, suspecting I'd be telling the story over and over.

We'd reached the building where Aunt Gill lived. Cass and I walked into the entryway. I thought again about how like and how unlike this was to the YWCA. I knocked on the door, and Gill opened it.

"Bet! You're back!" She engulfed me in a huge hug and pulled me inside. Cass followed. "I'm so glad you made it back in one piece."

"Were you expecting otherwise?" I tilted my head.

"I had some help, but I'm afraid Morgan's lessons weren't

enough to prevent Rolf from cutting my neck and my hand as he stole my portal key."

"Oh, Bet!" My aunt embraced me once more. She stood back a little to examine my injuries with a hand and her eyes. "But if he took your key, how did you return?" We all walked into the kitchen.

I smiled slightly and sat down at the table. "With his. He'd lost the original at the restaurant where I worked to earn enough money to stay and look for him."

"Bet also brought back a young man," Cass said. He stood against the counter. "Shy, young Bet picked up a suitor."

"Oh, it isn't like that!" I glanced at Cass and then Aunt Gill. "Quint is from another world and he was sent to learn about the portals."

Cass smirked. "We left him with the council."

"Then you've heard all that transpired while you were gone?" My aunt held both of my hands in her own.

"Not the details, but yes."

"And now you must tell us what happened to you and how you found Rolf." She stared into my eyes.

I glanced at Cass. "I'm afraid I have to report that the red apples didn't work quite the way we expected. The first led me to a meteorite, a huge rock that was alien to Earth. And it wasn't the only thing that didn't belong there. The world seemed to be full of them."

Cass rubbed his chin. "I hadn't considered that

there would be other people or items on this 'Earth' that weren't native there. That's very interesting."

"What about the other apples?" Aunt Gill's keen eyes urged me to continue.

"The second, well..." I shook my head, feeling a flush creep up my face. "Suffice it to say it was wasted. And the third led me to Quint, who was a customer at the restaurant. But then, so was Rolf." I blinked. "There must have been something about the place that drew us all there. Perhaps it was the name, Satellite. I got the impression they called the moon that circled their world a satellite. And did I tell you they called the city The Big Apple?"

"Interesting. But you found Rolf in the end." Cass' shoulders lifted in a shrug.

"Yes, or rather he found me. That's where it became difficult." I shuddered remembering my time with him. "He wanted me to help him purchase poisons to bring back here, and he also wanted my key since he'd lost his own."

"And you were cut fighting with him." Aunt Gill pushed my head back so she could look at my neck more closely. "It doesn't look too bad."

"My friend Carolyn tended to it, and to my hand. Quint saw that Rolf had me in his clutches and brought her and a few others from the restaurant to help me get away from him, but Rolf took the green apple along with the poisons."

Aunt Gill sighed and led me to a chair. "You must know that I hadn't intended for you to have such a treacherous time on your first mission."

I nodded. "I don't blame you for shoving me out of the nest too soon." I tried to smile and thought about how I'd felt every time I had to find a solution to a problem. "I was angry at you every time I was in a predicament when I could have used more training. But I did it my way. And I made it back. Now I can see why you do it, why you're so willing to help the council."

"Do you still want to go back to the farm?" she asked.

I sighed. "Not before we rescue Morgan. And I can't leave Quint to find his way back to his home alone!"

CHAPTER 18.

Aunt Gill handed me a cup of tea. "Quint is the young man you brought back with you?"

"Yes." I held the steaming cup but didn't bring it to my lips. Should I mention the questions I'd had since Monique told me the story she was writing? "There's something else. Could I see the book that Fiona used as a model for the dress she made?"

"Why would you want to see that when there are so many more important things to worry about?" Aunt Gill took a good look at me and my clothes. Like Cass, she frowned. "And, by the way, what are you wearing?"

I looked down at the shirt and jeans and chuckled. "This is what the young women wear on Earth."

"But what happened to the clothes you had, including that dress?"

I bit my lower lip. "I left them behind. But they're safe." I hoped she wasn't angry. "I believe the dress will be the model for the one in the book. I don't know how that can be, but Monique was writing a book that sounded like the one Fiona described. Is it a common story?"

My aunt shook her head.

Cass silently leaned against a wall all this time, but seemed to understand. "Maybe what she's saying is this book is being written by someone Bet met on Earth."

"Yes, Cass, that's exactly what I think. The young woman who shared a room with me in the place I stayed was writing a novel. Quint comes from the place where the book may have been before someone brought it here, perhaps Clare. So, somehow, we have to get him back to Earth so he can take a copy home with him for Clare to find. In the past, if that's possible." I stopped. "I'm not making sense, but that's the only way it could have happened."

My aunt's eyebrows converged over her nose. "Clare already found it."

I scratched my ear. "Yes, that's one part I don't understand. And Monique hadn't finished writing it."

Cass stood straighter. "Remember, Gillian, when you journeyed, it wasn't only from one world to another. We've all traveled through time, both backwards and forwards. The portals take us both ways. We've remarked it was the same time of day on either side of the portal, but not necessarily the same point in time. It is possible that Bet is correct."

Gill nodded and looked at my untouched cup. "Well, you must be hungry and tired."

I stifled a yawn. "I *was* up all night. Sometime I must tell you about the foods I ate on Earth, and served to others, but right now, I want to know what anyone's doing to find Morgan. Leone and Angus didn't say."

"The council sent Conner Royce two days ago to try to find out where Orson and his men took him, but Conner hasn't returned."

I shook my head. "Why didn't they mention that when we were in the council chambers?"

Cass shrugged. "I'm certain they believe that it's not your affair."

"But Morgan was my trainer! I was the one who allowed Rolf to return to Nokar with the poisons." My hands shook and my breathing rate increased. "What if he uses them on Morgan? It's my responsibility to rectify the situation."

A knock echoed through the room. Aunt Gill opened the door to Leone and Quint.

Leone stepped over the threshold. "Quint expressed a desire to see you again before we send him home."

I smiled to see his pleasant face again. "Quint, this is my aunt, Gillian Talbot."

He inclined his head. "How do you do?"

"Better, now that my niece has returned." She

turned to Leone. "Any word from Connor?"

Leone shook her head.

Cass looked from Aunt Gill to Leone and back again. "You realize that if Rolf has joined Orson, they not only have the poisons but a way to leave Nokar."

I slapped a hand to my mouth. "My apple key!"

"Quite so, Bet."

"They could have gone to Earth! But why?" My mind whirled. "It's such a large and crowded place. How will we ever find them? Even if they're in the Big Apple."

"The what?" My aunt stared at me.

"That's what they call the city where we were. It's really called New York."

Quint nodded, but then frowned. "Maybe Rolf will take them to the restaurant."

I shook my head. "If he thinks I'm still there, it's the last place he'd take them. You saw how the staff helped me. They know what he did to me." I sighed. "I'd guess he'd try to get as far away as possible while he plans, although they could still be on Nokar where they know their way around."

Quint looked at me. "But we're agreed that they're in one of two worlds, right?"

I shrugged.

"Unless they stole another portal key." Cass' smile was strained.

Aunt Gill gasped, "I hadn't thought of that."

Leone shook her head. "We have to act on the assumption that they're here or used the apple to go to Earth."

This was still so new to me. "What options are the council considering?"

"One thing we can't do is wait for Royce to return," Leone replied. "We must act immediately. I'm afraid you'll have to return to the council with me after all, Bet, and tell them all you know about Earth. We need that information if they've gone to Earth."

I stiffened. They'd sent me off saying they would ask Quint about it. "Didn't Quint tell you? I doubt I can add anything to what he said."

Leone shook her head. "We were too busy asking him about his own land, his portal key and why he was sent to Earth."

"But I thought...even you said..." I turned my attention to Gill. "It was Clare, wasn't it, who went to Lamady?"

Leone nodded. "She was never able to make contact with the rulers, only to tell a few of the natives about our world and the portals."

I was still worried overmuch about the book and trying to grasp the sequence of events. "Are they the ones who gave her the book?" I looked from Leone to my aunt and back.

"Book?" Leone appeared confused but no one

explained.

"I don't know. We'd have to check her report." Cass stroked his chin.

"If Quint brings the book back from Earth, how will it get to whoever gave it to Clare?" I wondered aloud. "Somehow that has to be before Clare arrives."

"What are you talking about?" Leone asked.

We told her about the book Clare brought back and gave to the dressmaker.

"Ah, yes, I remember something about that in her report, but it seemed so trivial." Leone shook her head.

Cass' full eyebrows rose at least an inch. "Bet is right. Something is very strange about all of this."

"Perhaps Quint shouldn't return to Lamady to tell his people about the portals, Earth, and Nokar." Aunt Gill gazed through narrowed eyes at the young man.

"That can't be!" Quint shook his head violently. His eyes blazed.

I put a hand on his arm. "We're just speculating, trying to make sense of what we know."

Cass asked Quint. "Would those you'll report to purposely avoid meeting with Clare because of what they learn from you?"

Quint's rapid breath slowed as he thought it through. At last he shook his head. "They're not like that. They might not like what they consider magic, but perhaps they'd welcome contact with other worlds and be curious about the people and customs. And I won't report to the Mothers anyway, but to my sister."

Leone ignored his last sentence and tilted her head. "Unless someone poisoned their minds against us."

Quint shook his head violently. "I'd never do that!"

I reached out a hand and placed it on his shoulder. "I'm sure Leone didn't mean you, Quint."

He nodded at my reassurance. "Then what did you mean?"

Leone shrugged.

I bit my lip.

"Bet, do you have something in mind?" Cass stroked his chin.

"Well, could Orson or Rolf find a way to Quint's world? If they contacted the rulers, who knows what lies they'd spread. Of course, they'd go there to avoid the council, to go some place they didn't think the council could go or would think to look for them."

Cass' brows shot up again and he nodded. "That is a possible scenario."

"But how would they get to Lamady?" Aunt Gill shook her head. "I still think the likely place for them to be is right here on Nokar."

Leone started for the door. "We can't know for certain unless you attempt to follow them."

Cass hung back. "And how do you propose we do that?"

Leone stopped and grimaced. "We've had no luck with our scout so far, but if two people each go to Earth and Lamady, and the rest of us scour Nokar, we have a chance of finding them."

Quint held up his three-pronged fork and looked pointedly at me. "I can take someone back with me to Lamady, but I'm not sure my key will work from here."

I nodded. "I'd love to see your land. What about the portal key Clare used to go there?"

Leone's eyes opened wide. "Yes, we'll have to find it."

Aunt Gill's mouth pressed together in a line. "Except we don't know when or where that would take any of us."

"We should locate it," Cass told Leone. "There's a chance Orson took it."

"Or that someone did, not necessarily Orson. I still doubt he would want to go to Lamady." I couldn't imagine that. It was an even stranger destination for him than Earth.

"If he did, how could we follow?" Quint's voice rose as it tended to do when he became anxious.

"You can go back to Earth with the hat and then use your fork," I suggested.

"Then we have our plan." Leone opened the door. "We find the key to Lamady. If it's there, two of you will use it and two can go to Earth."

Cass stared at her. "Do you mean for me to travel again after all these years?"

"One person couldn't carry out the mission alone," Aunt Gillian said.

I didn't point out that I'd done that.

"Cass, it hasn't been that long. And if the key is missing, you'll all go to Earth, and two of you will continue on to Lamady."

We left my aunt's apartment. As we walked quickly back to the council chambers, Quint managed to stay beside me, giving me the perfect opportunity to ask my questions about him and his world, or as Andre called it, his planet.

"Tell me again why the Mothers sent you to find out about the portals."

Quint shrugged. "I told you; they weren't the ones. My sister sent me because I was more willing to go than my brothers."

"Do you have a position in the ruling government?"

Quint gasped. "Of course not! Lamady isn't like your world. Our council consists of the oldest and wisest women of our people. They hold court in the capital, Dalam. The men serve them in any way they desire."

"But they didn't demand that one or more of your brothers use the fork? And while I'm asking, how did anyone know the fork was a portal key?"

He sighed. "It's a long and rather boring story. I

doubt you'll want to hear it all. Suffice it to say, my brothers begged for less dangerous tasks, beginning with the eldest. And since I am the youngest it fell to me. My sister, Zara, found the fork or was given it. She would have been a council member except that she's always kept to herself, appearing irregularly to make pronouncements which the council sometimes follows. But she and my mother have a...difficult relationship."

"So Zara's a wiser woman than your wise women?"

"I suppose you might say that." He grinned. "She dabbles in magic."

CHAPTER 19.

We'd reached the building housing the council before we finished making our plans. Aunt Gill continued to reassure me we'd finish them as we needed, although I'd come to doubt her reassurances based on my recent experiences. Leone led the way up the stone steps, through the double doors and across the marble hall to the chamber. When we entered, the other councilors looked up from their long table.

"We've come for the key Clare used to travel to Lamady," Leone said. "Is it still in the vault? We'll also need her notes."

Liam rose. "I'll go look." He slipped through a narrow side door, but returned moments later, his brow and mouth constricted. "The key's gone."

Leone strode to the council table. "Orson may have taken it. If he did, we can guess where he went. I suggest we send a party to search for him."

Liam gripped the table as he sat again. "But

without the key, how will the search party get there?"

My aunt stood beside Leone. "By way of Earth using Quint's key from there to Lamady." She looked back to Quint and me. "Bet and I will accompany him."

"You're forgetting something." Cass leaned against the door jamb. "Clare's key took her to another time in Lamady history."

I'd been thinking about that. "We don't know exactly when in Lamady history, but she traveled there before she left your service. We can travel to Lamady with Quint and perhaps that will take us early enough to wait for Orson's arrival. Did Clare report where the portal led?"

The councilors whispered among themselves for a few minutes, while we waited. When I could bear it no longer I asked, "Why won't you tell us what you know? It's important, especially to those who go after Orson."

Angus nodded. "You must understand, the council has kept so many secrets over the years, it is difficult for us to share what we know, even with our own travelers. From the time the portals were first discovered, the council has collected any information we could about their operation, but often, I'm afraid, we only told the travelers what we deemed important for them to know. We may have erred on the side of withholding too much." He turned to the other councilors, and they nodded.

I looked at my aunt. Had she undertaken quests without full knowledge in the past? Did that happen often? So I wasn't the only one?

She frowned but didn't say anything.

Cass cleared his throat as he stood up straighter. "It's about time you told those in the most danger what they're up against. This is one of the reasons I decided I would travel no longer. Have you even discovered how the portals were formed, or by whom? How they work?"

Aunt Gillian frowned. "We've always assumed you'd tell us everything we needed to know to achieve each mission, but perhaps that's not the case. Perhaps you haven't realized that lack of knowledge could jeopardize our efforts."

Leone joined the others at the table taking her usual seat.

Angus let out a breath. "Yes, this time I believe you have a right to know all that we do." His gaze shifted again to the other councilors. "The portal key that Clare used was in the form of a seashell."

I gasped.

Leone stared at me. "What is it, child?"

I swallowed, loud enough for others to hear since they stared at me. "I...I had a dream before I left the farm about a seashell that took me to a beach."

"Precisely. Clare arrived on a beach." Angus' eyes widened.

Quint shrugged. "I could have told you that. More than half of Lamady is water and there are many beaches.

I left from one myself."

"So how will we know where Orson will arrive?" I asked.

"Wait." Leone rose again and walked through the narrow door Liam used. When she returned, she waved a sheaf of papers. "This is Clare's full report. It's not very detailed about places, only those she met. But she says..." She looked through the pages until she found what she was looking for. "Here it is. She says: 'the sand is white like that at Marto Bay, and the water is almost green. The sun beat down on me so I rushed for the shelter of the overhanging rocks'."

"She's describing the beach at Richy Isle." Quint grinned. "It's the only one with high hills nearby. Jonica Harbor is also surrounded by mountains but the sand is black."

"OK." I smiled slightly that Cass had adapted the term. "So we know where to go. If we return with you by way of Earth, can you get us there?"

Quint's face clouded. "Well, it's not easy to reach from Dalam City." Then his eyes cleared. "If we can hire a boat, we can sail there."

"There may be more in Clare's report to help you." Leone handed the papers to Aunt Gill.

"When do we leave?" I started for the door.

"Bet, not so quickly." My aunt put a restraining hand on my arm. "We have to plan carefully what we'll do when we capture Orson and his men."

"I thought...I mean..." My shoulders slumped. "He'll have the key, right? So we bring them back here."

Leone steepled her fingers. "It took a force of ten to chase him from the capital. You are only three."

"Ah, but we have a secret weapon," Aunt Gill said.

I stared at her. "We do?"

"Actually we have more than one." She squeezed Cass' shoulder. "We have a wizard." Then she rested the other hand on Quint's shoulder. "And we have a native of Lamady, one with some resources I would guess." She tilted her head and looked at him with wide eyes.

"Oh! I suppose so." Quint's mouth twisted into a frown.

"Quint, what haven't you told us?" I demanded.

"Well, I...my mother is one of the ruling Mothers."

I should have remembered that. But his sister sent him to Earth. "Would your mother help us? Or the other ruling Mothers?"

He pressed his lips together and swallowed hard. "I guess I can ask."

I wondered about their relationship. "What if we give her information about the portals?"

He nodded. "That might help, although she wasn't too keen on sending anyone." A laugh burst from him. "I'm not even sure she knows where I am."

"You'll talk to her. I suppose that's the most we can

hope." Angus studied him. "And if the Mothers won't help?"

"There's always Zara, my sister."

I nodded. "The person who found the key and gave it to you."

Leone handed the hat I'd retrieved on Earth to Aunt Gill. "Be safe."

"I guess there's no time for more than a general plan. We'll go immediately." My aunt led the way out. "We need to take weapons."

It was a market day. People and wagons filled the street. We weaved our way through the crowds, first for a stop at Gill's and then at Cass' house.

As we started for the harbor, I thought about the difficulties of getting the four of us through the portal. I could duck under General Mundsen's horse in the evening after most people had left, and no one saw Quint and me reappear there in the early hours of the morning when we came from New York. But it was now broad daylight. Neither Aunt Gill nor Cass could unobtrusively make their way under the horse, not with children and adults about.

"How will we all travel to Earth together?" Quint seemed to read my mind. "The space under that statue is low and small, and there are now four of us."

Cass smiled at him. "I've thought about that. It's very simple. We won't."

"What?" I stopped walking and stared at him. "But

then how will we get to Earth?" Aunt Gill and Quint turned to Cass.

"We learned a long time ago that every portal has a complementary one." As usual, he sounded like a teacher when he talked.

I slapped a hand to my mouth. "That's what Rolf meant when he said there was more than one on Earth."

Cass nodded. "Exactly. I believe the counterpart to the portal you used is another statue, created by the same sculptor, from the material he removed from the stone as he created the general's monument."

"Is that why he paid more attention to sculpting the horse than the general?" I asked.

"Oh, I doubt it. He didn't know he was creating a portal, may not have even known they exist." Cass chuckled. "We still know so little about them. But he loved animals."

"What and where is this other statue?" Aunt Gill asked.

Cass grinned. "Follow me." He strode down the brick street toward the harbor, but not to the center of the plaza. Instead, he led us to the left side and a statue of a huge bear. I was surprised there weren't any children climbing all over it, but the crowds still surrounded General Mundsen and his horse.

The bear stood on its hind legs, front paws up as if to spring on unsuspecting prey, quite lifelike, even though it was the same dark gray stone as the General's statue. The portal wasn't obvious until Cass stood in front of the beast and we saw the sheer size. Five men could walk abreast between the bear's legs.

I walked toward the space clutching the hat in one hand and my aunt's arm in the other. She in turn held Quint's hand and he held onto Cass. As we passed underneath, the familiar lack of sensations enveloped us. Nothing to see, smell or hear for a moment, and then we stood on a street corner. I recognized it immediately. We stood across from the entrance to the park that Carolyn and I passed through my first day in New York.

"Quint, can you find the portal to your world from here?" Aunt Gill asked.

He smiled. "Yes. I know exactly where we are."

"Wait!" I held up my hand. "We have to go to the Y."

My aunt stared at me, hands on hips. "Bet, there's no time to visit your friends."

"No, you don't understand. It's the book. The one Clare brings back. We have to get a copy from Monique and bring it to Lamady."

Quint looked puzzled. "I thought Monique hadn't finished it yet."

He was right, and still I couldn't see how else the book would be there for Clare if we didn't deliver it.

Cass chuckled. "Bet, don't worry. There has to be a

way to make it happen."

"Oh, alright." I pressed my lips together, and my shoulders sagged, as I finally let go of that obsession.

Aunt Gill raised her eyebrows. "So, Quint. The portal?"

"Yes. This way." He pointed straight ahead and stepped off the curb to cross the street, but stopped when he saw the oncoming traffic. "I forgot about all the automobiles."

Cass stroked his beard and watched them pass, but my aunt tapped her foot. Neither seemed surprised by the vehicles. The light changed.

"We can cross now," I said.

Quint led us into the park. "The portal isn't far." True to his word, he stopped in front of an underpass, where the walking path went beneath a roadway. "This is it." He took out the fork and we joined hands as we did on Nokar. "Ready?"

We stepped forward as one. The cessation of sound and sight were similar to what I felt before. That nothingness I associated with portals. Then we exploded onto a sandy beach, surrounded by large rocks.

"I left from here, but it's not the beach we're looking for. The center of the city is this way." Quint walked away from the water and we followed.

CHAPTER 20.

We walked through huge double doors into a vast room. The gloomy hall rose to unseen heights. Lit only by torches at intervals along each wall, it stretched the length of a city block in New York. Even all the torches didn't illuminate the other end. In the center of the chamber stood a raised dais with a round wooden table surrounded by eight heavy chairs, lit by a chandelier hanging by a long chain. The women sitting in those chairs rose as one and turned to look at us.

One came forward, tall, with pale blond hair twisted into a braid down her back. Her red and gold gown whooshed as she moved, the only sound in the room, and the jewels across the bodice reflected the chandelier light. "Quint! You've returned." Her voice sounded like a flute, high-pitched and melodic. "And who are these people you've brought with you?"

"Mother, I met them during my travels. This is Bet, that is..." He cleared his throat. "Anabet Haines, her aunt

Gillian Talbot and Mr. Cass." He turned to us. "My mother, Mother Lyra."

"Cass Holden, m'lady." The short man bowed to Quint's mother, making me smile.

Mother Lyra frowned. "Zara told us she sent you on that fool's errand. Are these people from the land you found?"

"Oh, no!" Quint swallowed and began his story. "The place I went to with Zara's key is called Earth by the inhabitants. These friends are from Nokar, another world." His hand motioned to me. "I first met Bet on Earth. She arrived not long after I did, and told me her people know much about the portals. I returned with her to Nokar to learn more and brought them here to tell you. Please hear them out."

We were there for another reason, but Quint knew his mother and I didn't. He'd tell her the story the best way to get her to help.

Mother Lyra had piercing blue eyes and a pleasant face like Quint. She examined each of us with a penetrating gaze and then addressed her son. "And what do they want in return?" Nothing would get past her.

Aunt Gillian stepped forward. My aunt might be the only one who could match wits with shrewd Mother Lyra. "We believe several men from our world passed through a portal to yours, and we must bring them back."

Her eyebrows arched. "Criminals you mean."

"Some would call them rebels, but they're traitors and would kill sooner than negotiate with their enemies. You wouldn't want them to remain here, and we want to bring them to justice."

"And you think we'll help you find them?" The smile on Mother Lyra's face never reached her eyes.

"Oh, we know where they'll be at some point. All we'll need is a way to get there." Gill held Lyra's stare.

Quint stepped forward. "Mother, these men will land on the beach at Richy Isle."

"If they can get there, why can't you?" She was only asking Aunt Gill.

My aunt answered as if she knew it would come. "Because there is only one key that leads there and they have it. We didn't have time to make another."

"So these 'keys' can be manufactured?"

Cass spoke up. "They can be...devised."

Lyra glanced at Cass, then turned back to her son. "Magic. They use magic to create them."

The color drained from Quint's face. "Mother, you know there are uses for magic as long as they are limited. The key Zara found and gave me to test was magic too, you know. You objected when she first showed it to you, but it worked very well."

She frowned at him, then looked at us. "I'm sorry, but I can't help you." She turned and walked back to the table, her clothes swishing and her steps ringing on the stone floor.

"But Mother..."

She turned her head. "You heard me, Quint. Your friends can return to their Nokar. We will not help them."

Quint's jaw clenched as he turned to us. "We have one other option." His voice was a whisper. He pushed the doors open and we followed him out onto the marble steps leading down to the large, sunlit square. I had to shade my eyes.

"Where are we going now?" Cass asked.

"To my sister. Zara." Quint walked quickly down the steps. We followed as he turned right. The building we'd been in and those nearby were made of large stone blocks instead of the brick in Willoughby or the glass and steel in New York City, with narrow alleys between them.

He led us down one of the alleys. "I don't know how Zara knew what the key was, but then, she's a witch."

"But you said she was wise." I grabbed his arm and forced him to look at me. "You're taking us to a witch so that she'll help us?"

"As you might have guessed, the Mothers frown on the use of magic. Those who use it are considered witches and not allowed to participate in our society." We'd reached the end of the alley. Smaller buildings spread out before us. "Her place is this way."

We passed the last buildings and came to an open field with a copse of trees to one side. Quint led us to the wood. As we neared, we could see it was bigger and thicker than it appeared from far away. A series of low buildings were hidden by the trees. He knocked on the door of one and it opened.

The woman in the doorway resembled Mother Lyra, but was much younger. Her golden hair curled around her face and her blue eyes smiled at Quint. She rushed to embrace him. "Welcome back, dear brother." Her voice was even more melodic than her mother's.

"Zara, I'd like you to meet my friends." He turned halfway and once more introduced us.

This time, we were welcomed warmly. "Any friend of Quint's is mine as well."

"Your key took me to a world called Earth, where I met Bet. Her people on Nokar have traveled through the portals for a long time."

Zara grinned and practically danced with excitement. "I knew it! I knew there were more portals. Hadn't I told you so?" she asked Quint.

"I expect one reason Mother wouldn't allow you to use the fork was to prevent anyone from learning there was a portal here, so no one could come this way." Quint looked down. "And now I've brought people here from another world."

"I think you're right about Mother." Zara nodded.

That didn't quite agree with what I knew. "But why wouldn't she help us?"

"What did you ask of her?" Zara said.

"Traitors from our world are coming to yours, and we're here to bring them back." Aunt Gill shook her head. "But they'll arrive on a beach that Quint says is hard to reach."

He nodded. "The beach on Richy Isle."

Zara rubbed her chin. "That's only approachable by boat."

"And that's what we need. But your mother refused to help."

"Well, that's easily remedied." Zara smiled broadly. "I'll provide a boat and two of my men can accompany you."

"How can we thank you?" Aunt Gill took Zara's hands.

"By telling me about the portals, at least enough so I can create more." A beguiling smile accompanied her words. "You can remain here long enough to do that."

Aunt Gill and Cass exchanged a look. Cass shook his head. "I'm afraid we can't, not because we don't want to, but because we don't know how the portals formed."

"Oh." She frowned. "But where are my manners? Come inside and we'll have tea while you tell me whatever you can." The ornate wood chairs in the first room we came to had maroon brocade-covered seats. Matching draperies framed every window. She led us to a pair of maroon and white striped couches, facing each other across a low table. "Please sit."

A young woman appeared in a doorway at the back of the room. Shorter than Zara, she had light blue eyes and pale hair, almost white.

"Please bring us some tea, Mila."

"Yes, m'lady." The woman curtsied slightly and left again only to appear a few minutes later with a tray of teacups and saucers and a white porcelain pot. She poured us each a cup, looking at us with thinly veiled curiosity and then left.

"So tell me, how many portals are there?" Zara asked. She sipped her tea and sat back to listen. The combination of her stare and voice mesmerized me.

"There are over seventy that we know of," Aunt Gill began. She and Cass told Zara much more than I knew about the portals. I wasn't surprised they revealed so much to her. I wanted to tell her everything I knew, too. Although I thought Cass, at least, wouldn't be so susceptible to her charms.

"We're continually finding more portals as well as the keys to work them," he said.

"Cass can devise a key, given enough time and some knowledge of where the portal might lead," I blurted, then clapped a hand over my mouth.

We ran out of things to tell Zara the same time we finished our tea. She rose and rang a little bell sitting on a table at her side. Mila returned and cleared the tea service without a word. As she walked away, Zara called to her. "Please ask Dent and Fallon to join us. And prepare a day's provisions for our guests to take with them."

"Yes, m'lady." The curtsy was deeper this time.

Aunt Gill watched her go and then faced our hostess. "Zara, we've revealed much to you about the portals. Would you tell us where you obtained the fork Quint used?"

Zara glanced toward the doorway Mila went through and sighed. "Mila is a Karene."

Quint gasped. "I didn't know." He turned to us. "The Karene were exiled by the Mothers because they practice magic. They live on Richy Isle, but the other side from the beach you wish to go to."

Zara nodded. "She obtained the fork from her people and told me only a little of what it could do."

Before she could tell us more, two men dressed in trousers made from animal hides and linen shirts with wide sleeves, entered the room. One was tall and slim with broad shoulders and a scarred face. His bright blue eyes took in all of us. The other was shorter and broader, with black hair and a mustache, and warm brown eyes.

"You will accompany my brother and his friends to the beach on Richy Isle. Use the largest boat, and make sure you have blankets. Mila is preparing provisions."

Both men clapped a fist to their chests and bowed slightly. We followed them out and through the trees to a rocky shore where three large row boats were pulled up out of the water.

"I'll go collect the supplies," the taller man, Fallon, said. When he returned, we all pushed the largest boat into the water and got in.

"How far is it?" I asked Quint.

"We should be there while it is still daylight."

I watched the land recede as the two men rowed the boat far out onto the calm blue green sea, hoping we could trust them as much as I trusted Quint.

CHAPTER 21.

We reached Richey Isle faster than expected and climbed out of the boat onto the sandy shore. The sun began it's descent. The beach was completely deserted, except for some yellow, sparrow-like birds circling overhead.

The only beach I'd ever seen had been rocky, not like this one. A wide strip of sand, soft and as white as snow, curved around the face of a gray mountain. Quint had been right about how difficult it would be to reach without a boat.

"So we just wait here for Orson and his men to arrive?" I felt unsure what would happen.

Aunt Gill nodded. "I hope it won't be long."

"And what do we do then? We have no plan." I faced my aunt with arms crossed.

"We rescue Morgan and get the poisons, of course." Still not specific.

Cass stroked his chin. "I believe Bet wants to know

how we'll do that. We don't know how many men Orson has."

"I expect you have magic to use in situations like this." Quint pulled out the blanket Zara gave us and spread it on the sand. The intricately woven pattern in gold and blue contrasted with the whiteness of the beach.

"Perhaps. But I'll need each of you to do your part in fighting them."

I fingered my knife as I sat down cross-legged and Cass joined me. My eyes followed Aunt Gill, who paced up and down the strand, each step made difficult by the shifting soft white powder. Quint helped the two guards pull the boat onto shore.

My aunt finally stopped near the blanket and looked down at us. "Perhaps we should find some place where they won't see us immediately. The element of surprise could help."

Quint shook his head. "There are no caves in the mountain, not even a pass." He glanced up at the cloud-free turquoise sky. In the next hour or so it would darken as the sun set, hopefully not before the men arrived. "We don't need a shelter, only somewhere to hide." He looked up and down the shore, then back at the sheer gray stone behind us.

Fallon approached Quint, frowning. "The tide's coming in, sir. We'll bring the boat in further, and you'll have to move your friends closer to the mountain."

Quint nodded and stood.

Cass smiled. "I have an idea. We can put the boat on its side, and settle in behind it. That will give us a little protection and prevent anyone from discovering us too soon."

Quint and the guards brought the boat closer, and Aunt Gill folded the blanket. Cass and I removed our tracks in the sand. Soon the six of us were ensconced on the mountain side of the upturned boat.

To pass the time, I asked my aunt for Clare's report. "Perhaps there's more in it telling how she obtained Monique's book."

She handed the sheaf of papers to me, and I began to read. "Listen to this. 'When I returned to the beach, a boat was coming into shore. There were three women in it, all as short as I am. Two had long, white-blond hair and pale eyes but the other had very short hair, almost black, and oddly slanted eyes'." I looked up at Gill. "That sounds like Monique! But it couldn't be, could it? How would she get here?"

"It would explain where Clare got the book," Gill said.

Cass rubbed his chin. "Every explanation we find leads to even more questions."

I couldn't sit still, so I took out the provisions Quint's sister gave us. I nibbled on some bread and cheese, still thinking about Clare's report, but couldn't bring myself to eat another apple. How long would we have to wait? "What are the chances that the men will come to this place at this time?" I should have asked that before.

"There are places and times that seem to bring people together." Cass' eyes held a speculative look. "Just as you, Quint and Rolf were at the restaurant on Earth at the same time, the men we are seeking might very well arrive here this evening even though they left Nokar earlier than we did."

A length of the beach was visible to us but we were hidden by the boat from anyone approaching. I didn't dare stand. Instead I shifted position every once in a while. Aunt Gill caught my eye and frowned. Resigned to stay in one place, I tried to relax.

"Do you think we can overcome them, just the six of us?" My mouth could move even if I couldn't.

"With the element of surprise on our side, we should be able to." Quint forced a smile. "Relax, Bet. Dent and Fallon are two of Zara's best guards. Your aunt is well-trained, and Mr. Cass has a few tricks up his sleeves." He turned to the older man. "Am I right?"

Cass scratched his tilted head. "Well, I do have a few ideas. Bet, how far did your training with Morgan progress, Bet?"

"We worked on knife skills and one-on-one fighting." I shook my head. "I'm not very good."

Aunt Gill patted my hand. "Nonsense, Bet. You did

admirably well with your lesson."

"But I only had one. I wasn't even able to fight Rolf off on Earth."

The heat of the day waned as the sun descended to the blue-green horizon of the ocean. A light wind carried the salty scent from the sea. We took turns peeking around the boat. Suddenly, from out of nowhere, eight men appeared at the water's edge, as if they'd popped out of thin air. Was that what it looked like to anyone catching a glimpse of someone coming through a portal? One of the men was Morgan, bound at the hands and feet, looking thinner and paler than when I'd last seen him. He was held by a slim man with broad shoulders and a fierce expression. His eyes were dark and piercing, and his hair was dark as well. Rolf, in the same white shirt and black pants he'd worn on Earth, stood next to him. Memories of my last encounter with Rolf filled me with dread.

"Orson and his people." Aunt Gill whispered in my ear.

"Where are we?" Rolf looked around. "And where do we go now?"

Orson's head turned this way and that. "We can stay here, but we'll need supplies while we plan how to use the poisons you brought back to wrest power from the council." Orson pointed. "There's a boat. Perhaps we can use it." He led the others in our direction, dragging Morgan by the restraints on his wrists.

Dent put a finger to his lips, then counted silently, holding up the fingers of his right hand one at a time. When he reached five, he mouthed the word 'now', and we rose as one, pushing the boat over.

Cass murmured to himself, while the rest of us moved around the boat to take on the newcomers.

CHAPTER 22.

Fallon, drew his sword and swung it at a heavy-set man, who side-stepped the blow. I didn't see what happened next because I was too busy in hand-to-hand combat with Rolf. After what he'd done on Earth, I was determined to even the score. This time I'd prepared myself for his moves.

He grabbed at both my hands, but I pulled my left one free. His arm tightened around my neck, making breathing difficult. I kicked at his shins the way Morgan demonstrated in his training room, and he lost his grip on my right hand. I clutched my fists together but before I could swing around and hit him, he reached out and yanked my hair.

"Ouch!"

Morgan called to me, "Bet, shift."

I remembered what he meant and got the man off balance by shifting my own weight in a direction he didn't expect. My hands and feet focused on what I had to do, but my ears heard the shouts and cries from Aunt Gill and Quint.

Suddenly, the sand swirled in front of me, into the air. At first I thought the wind off the sea caused the spiral of particles, but then saw that the eddies were being controlled. Several of them went higher and higher, directed toward the eyes of Orson and his men, but not us. Cass! It had to be! Rolf raised his hands to protect his eyes. It gave me the opportunity to land a blow to his chin. As I did, Morgan freed himself from Orson's grip but still struggled with him.

From the corners of my eyes, I saw some of those in our party getting the upper hand. Fallon had the heavy-set man on the ground, and Quint held another of Orson's men. Aunt Gill struggled with a third man. They all had a difficult time steadying their legs enough in the shifting sand to land blows. They grasped at each other's bodies.

Morgan shouted at me. "Bet, your knife!"

I'd forgotten it, but felt the weight against the pocket of my jeans. I pulled it from its scabbard. Holding it the way he'd shown me, I slashed at Rolf's thigh, then whirled to use it on the arm of my aunt's opponent. He let go of her shoulder to defend himself. That was all she needed to renew her attack. I turned back to Rolf. Unfortunately the stab wound I'd inflicted on him wasn't enough to cripple him. He came at me, but lost his footing in the sand.

Lighter and nimbler, I could side-step him. The knife was still in my right hand. For the first time, I might have to take a life. Could I do that, even if Rolf wouldn't hesitate to kill me? He took his own knife out. I took a deep breath and moved my knife hand in an arc, aiming for his chest. The last of the sun's rays reflected off my knife into his eyes, and his hands automatically came up to defend his face. I cut his side more deeply than he'd cut me on Earth.

His blood reddened the white sand. He fell to his knees. Color drained from his face. His breath was ragged until, gasping for air, he fell over.

My first instinct was to go to him, to try to revive him, but a quick glance showed the others still hadn't completely subdued Orson's men, and Morgan, in his weakened state, was losing his fight with Orson. I rushed to his aid. Orson immediately attempted to overpower me with his larger size, but I stood fast, swept my knife through the air towards him with rapid strokes. Unfortunately none of them landed.

His eyebrows flew up, and his eyes glared.

We circled each other for a long time, feinting with our knives. I fought for my life, using moves I didn't know I knew. Bits and pieces of what Morgan taught me came together. The sun set, and it was dark on the beach. My legs tired from moving in the sand, and my hand on the knife handle cramped and slipped from sweat. Around me, bumps and scuffles indicated that the others still fought, too. The crash of waves on the sand grew fainter as the tide receded. When I lunged at him with an outstretched knife hand, he avoided the blade. Orson's grip on his knife let go, his hand probably as tired and sweaty as mine.

As Orson and I continued to fight, he pulled out a long, slender knife from a scabbard on his back. He wielded it with expert precision. With his longer arms and the length of the knife, he had an advantage. How could I even the odds? And where were Cass' spirals of sand when I most needed them?

I couldn't depend on help from anyone else. My heart pounded. I took a deep breath and charged, crouching a bit so Orson reached past me. I thrust my knife upward into his stomach.

"Why you...!" He panted but continued to stab at me with one hand as he tried to staunch the blood flowing from his belly with the other.

I ducked every jab, practically dancing around him, looking for my opening, gasping, then holding every breath I took. There it was. His right side was completely unprotected. I held the knife the way Morgan taught me and carefully threw it, aiming the point in line with where I expected his heart was. The blade reached its mark and he fell. I let out the breath I'd held for some time. Orson was no longer breathing when I reached him.

The knife was firmly embedded, but I pulled it out, then turned to see who needed my help. Orson's men stared at their fallen leader. They dropped their weapons.

We soon had them all subdued.

CHAPTER 23.

I felt nauseous thinking about what I'd done. How could I have killed a man? Two men. True, they would have killed me if I hadn't, but it still left me with a tight pain in my gut. I swallowed the bile that threatened to come up and looked around.

Aunt Gill rushed to Morgan's side to tend to him while Quint and his sister's men disarmed the rebels still alive. I swallowed again before touching Orson's clothes, but I had to reach inside to search for the green apple and the seashell. His body was cooling slowly. I found the two portal keys in the pockets of his trousers.

"Are these the poisons you mentioned?" Cass held up the drugstore bags he took from Rolf's pack.

I walked to him, opened one of the bags and peeked inside. "Yes." I looked up at Cass. "What can we do to destroy them?"

He rubbed his left ear. "Who says that we want to?"

I took out a bottle, the toilet cleanser, and waved it in front of him. "This is dangerous."

Cass chuckled. "It's a cleanser. Used in the right

way it's helpful." He rummaged in the two bags. "Most of these are likely superior to anything we have."

"So we should take them back to Willoughby?"

He shrugged. "Why not?"

Morgan, with support from Aunt Gill, joined us. "They tested one of the poisons on me. That one, I think." He pointed to the cleanser in my hand. "I knew enough to force myself to regurgitate as you do with most poisons, but enough entered my system to weaken me."

"You'll recover," Cass said. "I'm sure Gillian will be happy to play nursemaid until you're back to yourself." His eyes twinkled. The color rose in my aunt's cheeks.

I looked toward Quint. "I suppose we're finished here."

Aunt Gill nodded. "We can return to Nokar with the traitors and the poisons, and your friend can go home with his sister's guards and report on his adventures."

"But I promised him we'd tell him more about the portals." I crossed my arms.

She waved a hand in dismissal. "He knows enough for now." She walked toward the men. "We'll take the prisoners." Her voice was commanding and dismissive. "You can return to your capital."

Quint crossed his arms like I had and stood tall. "I'm not going back to Dalam. I'll return to Nokar with you and travel through more portals to see other worlds." He pressed his lips together. "Bet, tell your aunt I'm going with you."

"I've tried, Quint." I sensed his disappointment. "I wish you could. Maybe some day I'll return here, and we can go on another adventure."

He looked from one person to another, but no one offered to support his request. He gave it another try. "I helped you, didn't I? All of you. I've proven my worth. I won't go back to being my mother's errand boy or even my sister's."

Surprisingly, it was Cass who relented. "Perhaps he would be useful on Nokar." He stroked his chin. "I can use an assistant, who can learn to fashion portal keys and take over for me when I grow too old."

Quint's face lit up. "Really? That would be incredible. I promise you that you're not making a mistake."

"That's to be seen." Cass eyebrows rose. "It won't be easy, mind you."

Quint nodded, and I smiled at him.

Aunt Gill frowned. "If you're sure."

"Gillian, I believe the young man has some potential." Morgan cupped her chin. "I watched him fight with Orson's man Lister. Let Cass see what he can do with him."

Fallon and Dent put the boat back into the water. "Do you have a message for Lady Zara?" Dent asked Quint.

"Tell my sister I'll return once my knowledge of the

portals is sufficient for our use," he replied.

We watched them row off but lost sight of them when they rounded the headland.

"What do we do with Orson, Rolf and Lister's bodies?" I tried not to think about my part in killing two of them. "We can't leave their corpses here."

Aunt Gill studied the seashell we'd need to return to Nokar. "We'll take them back with us."

Cass, Quint and Morgan herded the rest of Orson's men into the small space where they'd first arrived. We helped move the bodies within the same area, then joined them. Cass and Quint touched the shell and the rest of us touched them so we were all transported through the nothingness. I didn't recognize the countryside where we landed.

Aunt Gill looked around through narrowed eyes. "I thought Leone said the portal was at the southern gate, but this is the western gate." She shrugged.

It wasn't a gate any more than a door. Instead, it was a wide space where several roads joined.

Aunt Gill and Morgan led our party toward the city. Cass brought up the rear, with Orson's men carrying their dead comrades. Quint and I walked in front of Cass, our shoes thumping on the brick pavement.

"Are you staying in Willoughby?" Quint asked. "Or will you travel again?"

I thought I knew why he asked. "I promised my

parents and brother I'd return home to our farm, at least for a visit."

He looked down so I couldn't tell but I thought he frowned.

"But I'll be back." It was a decision I hadn't made lightly. "If the council will still have me, I want to train to take over for my aunt someday."

He looked up and beamed. "Promise?"

I laughed at his eager face. "You haven't seen the last of me, Quint!"

The street narrowed as we neared the city center. The voices of other pedestrians mingled with the clip-clop of a few horses and the jangle of the wagons they pulled. The familiar sounds welcomed me home.

People we passed looked questioningly at the prisoners and the corpses they carried, but no one stopped us until we reached the building where the council met. We mounted the steps and entered. Aunt Gill and Morgan pushed open the doors to the council chamber.

The councilors sat at their table and looked up as we entered.

"Orson is dead," my aunt announced. "So are Rolf and Lister." She indicted the bodies that Orson's remaining men deposited on the floor.

We took turns describing what happened on the beach as Leone wrote down all we said. We also told the councilors about our visit to the Mothers and Zara.

Liam called two men to the chamber to take charge of the prisoners. A few others carried the bodies away.

I faced the councilors. "What will happen to Orson's men?"

Angus raised one eyebrow. "They'll be tried for treason. Cass, what have you there?"

"We retrieved the poisons Bet mentioned." Cass placed the bags on the table. "Our scientists should examine them, see whether they can duplicate the compositions and effects."

Leone nodded. She sighed. "And now, these two young people." She stared at me and Quint for a full minute before her stern countenance softened. "You've both proven yourselves useful."

Cass cleared his throat. "I'd like to take Quint on as an apprentice, if the council approves. See what sort of conjurer we can make of him."

She tapped her chin and raised an eyebrow. "And what of his homeland? Do they approve?"

"Some want me to learn all I can about the portals." Quint's voice quavered as he spoke, but he stood straight and tall. "Working with Mr. Cass will allow me to learn a great deal."

"And Bet?" Leone asked.

"I came here to train to take my aunt's place. I still have misgivings about what the council is doing, and I'd like to go home again if only for a visit. After all I've seen...and done, though, I want to see what else is out there on the other side of the portals. I only hope I'll be better prepared next time."

She nodded. "Duly noted. Gillian, do you approve?"

Aunt Gill looked at me, then addressed Leone. "Bet managed better than I did on my first assignment. I knew she had potential, but I'm convinced she has abilities we're only beginning to realize."

"I concur," Morgan said. "I'd like more time to train her and increase her confidence in her abilities."

"Then so be it." Angus rose and looked at me. "Welcome to the ranks of the Travelers of Nokar, Anabet Haines."

ABOUT THE AUTHOR

After retiring in 2008 after forty-five years in the scientific literature publishing business, Joyce Hertzoff moved from fact-based writing and the dreary mid-west to the sunny southwest where she and her husband love their mountain view and spicy food and she could flex her creative writing skills.

The Crimson Orb, the first novel in her Crystal Odyssey YA fantasy series, was published in June, 2014. Her flash mysteries, Natural Causes and Say Cheese were published in the anthologies *The Darwin Murders* and *Tasteful Murders*. A short story, Princess Petra, appears in *The Way Back* anthology.

Read more at: Website: http://joycehertzoffauthor.com

Book website: http://fantasybyjoycehertzoff.com

Made in the USA
Charleston, SC
28 October 2016